The Dim Light of Dawn

Hy Shaw

Published by Hayim Schwartzman, 2023.

THE DIM LIGHT OF DAWN

First edition. June 19, 2023.

Copyright © 2023 Hy Shaw.

ISBN: 979-8223200161

Written by Hy Shaw.

To my dear wife Anne who encourages me to go fishing.

ONE

June 2021—Saratoga Springs, New York

Gil peered over the dune and blushed with embarrassment. A young mother floated on the waves, breastfeeding her baby. The mother's eyes were closed, and she wore Mona Lisa's smile of contentment—just like the others. As far as Gil could see, there were waves full of women, all with their boobs and babies bobbing up and down. He felt mesmerized by the scene's tranquility.

Suddenly, the earth pulsed with a dull *thud thud*. The smell of fresh soil filled the air. Then, *crack crack*, off in the distance. *Thud thud*, right next to him. Leaves and dirt kicked up around him. Someone was shooting at him! He turned around and ran up the forested hill, hyperventilating, his feet slipping on the loose rocks and leaves. Bullets hit the ground all around him. He ran as fast as he could. Then he fell.

Gil woke with a start. He was breathing heavily and covered in a thin film of sweat, as usual. Lightning interrupted the darkness, and rain splattered against the windows. The clock on the bedside table said 4:05 a.m., so he shut off the alarm set for six. Although he always set his alarm, he never let it go off.

———————————

Gil once again went to work early. His workplace was a single-story metal building with an open floor plan, and from his workbench he continued trying to work the bugs out of a prototype manufacturing-line robot. Without the usual office chatter, he easily slipped into focused-work mode. Suddenly, he felt a hand on his shoulder and picked his face off the workbench. A yellow sticky note clung to his face, and his COVID mask was wet with drool.

"My office," Chet said. "Please."

The other workers watched as Gil followed Chet into his office. Chet shut the door.

"Gil, this is the third time this month I've found you asleep. I hope this means you're dating a younger woman."

Gil was too worked up to laugh. "I'm sorry, Chet. I guess I need to get some help with my sleep problem." He hesitated for a few seconds, not wanting to upset his friend. "By the way, I think I've decided to give you notice that I'm retiring. If I don't get healthier, I'm not going to live long enough to enjoy my retirement."

"Gil, I'm not asking you to leave. I just want—"

"Chet, this isn't about you. My health was going downhill even before Cyn died, and that just made it worse. I know I have a lot of work on my plate, so I'll give you six weeks' notice."

Chet plopped down into his chair. "Wow. We've been working together for over thirty years! I guess I really just want to support whatever's best for you." He thought for a moment. "Six weeks' notice is very generous of you, but you'll be hard to replace. Please write me a short retirement letter, and I'll get the ball rolling with HR. You know, this is probably going to get some of the other guys thinking about retirement too. Including me."

———

Gil and his coworkers were in the back room of a tavern just outside of town. The stained pine-board walls were covered with old local signs and photographs of people he didn't know. As Gil stood up to speak, he looked out at the small crowd and smiled. A few wore masks, but most, like Gil, had removed theirs while they enjoyed their libations. All of them were vaccinated and boosted, but COVID was still surging. "Our company was just a farm forty years ago, but it seems like it's been here forever. I've worked here almost since the beginning, and to me, it feels like home. Even though each of us is different from one another and comes from a different background, we're like a family. We work together as a team without even thinking about it, and we've accomplished some amazing things. Together, we've advanced the state of the art of robotics. Our company has done just about everything right, except for one thing."

Chet got a concerned look on his face.

"At every retirement party, we have beer and cake. People, cake does not go well with beer! I'd like my enduring legacy to this company to be the abolishment of this tradition. Your choice, beer or cake. Cheers!" The audience laughed and gathered around to wish him well.

TWO

Nurse Ivey had Gil sit on the side of the bed as she stuck sensors to his head, neck, and chest. The multitude of wires fed into a central hub on his chest, which then connected to the nurse's monitoring station via even larger cables. Gil could feel the weight of it.

"I'll be monitoring you remotely from the next room over there," the nurse said through a white N-95 mask. "You can read or watch TV until you're ready to sleep. Here's the TV remote. Use this controller to raise or lower the bed and to dim or shut off the lights. Use this button to call me if there's a problem or if you need to use the bathroom. Have a good night!"

Gil felt like a meatball in a bowl of spaghetti. There was no way he was going to fall asleep. He settled down and read several chapters of a science-fiction novel on his Kindle, then flipped through all the channels on the TV, feeling the despair that comes from finding only meaningless and uninteresting entertainment. He went back to the Kindle. After a while, he rang the button, and Nurse Ivey helped unplug him so he could use the bathroom. Then more of the same: reading and flipping channels on the TV, until he finally decided to try and sleep.

He stared at the ceiling for a while, then slowly and carefully tossed and turned, trying to get comfortable without disconnecting any sensors. This went on for what seemed like hours, when, suddenly, he woke up from a nightmare, breathing hard and covered in sweat. He turned on the light and raised the bed so he could sit. After a few deep breaths, he felt himself calming down, then turned off the lights and lowered the bed so he could stare at the ceiling some more.

He woke up again, but not from a nightmare. He just felt as though he wasn't going to sleep anymore. He turned on the light, raised the bed, and rang Nurse Ivey.

"Okay, it's almost six o'clock," she said. "You slept for a little more than two and a half hours. I'll get you unhooked."

"How'd I do?"

"Dr. Manomoney will review the data and discuss it with you at your next appointment."

––––––––––––––

Dr. Manomoney was a petite young woman who spoke with a lilting Indian-British accent that Gil found pleasant. She came across as very sharp and competent, but always cheerful. The room in her clinic was spartan, with two patient chairs, a rolling stool, and a computer terminal attached to an articulated wall mount. A poster about sleep apnea and one about relaxation techniques hung on the wall. "You slept enough during your study to give me a picture of what is going on," she said. "You do not have sleep apnea, which is both good news and bad news. It's good because it is a very serious condition, but it's bad because your type of insomnia is harder to treat than apnea.

"Because you've told me that falling asleep at night isn't usually your problem, I'd say that you have sleep-maintenance insomnia, which just means trouble staying asleep. I'd like to start you out with cognitive behavioral therapy for insomnia, or CBTI. I'll have you maintain a sleep log, and I'll meet with you about every week for ten weeks, guiding you with techniques to improve your sleep. Your case is special, however, because you've told me that you regularly have nightmares. You had one during your study last week, and it evoked a severe anxiety reaction. So before we start the CBTI, I'd like you to meet with Dr. Lipton, a psychologist, to see if he can determine what's causing your nightmares. In the meantime, let's start your sleep log, which may help Dr. Lipton too."

THREE

On Saturday morning, Gil drove over to his daughter Julia's house, and his son-in-law Mike waved to him from his lawn tractor. Two little faces appeared in the front window. Ziggy and Dez were jumping up and down, happy to see their Grampy. Julia opened the front door to let them out, and they dragged him to the swing set in the backyard. Ziggy was old enough to get himself swinging, so Gil focused on helping Dez into her swing while they giggled and chatted.

Mike shut off the tractor and walked over. "Hi."

"Hi." Gil pushed the girls a few more times. "I retired a few days ago."

"You what? For real?"

"Yup, for real." Gil gave him a big smile.

He came over and shook his hand. "Wow! What are you going to do?"

"Whatever I want! I decided that I need to spend more time on my health. I had a sleep study at the hospital a couple of weeks ago. I really need to fix my sleep problem. I also want to start exercising more. I could lose a few pounds—maybe more than a few. I'll need to get a few new hobbies too."

"Do Julia and Amelia know?"

"You're the first I've told. I'm going in to talk to Julia. I'll call Amelia today when she wakes up on California time. Maybe I'll go visit her soon." Ziggy leaped out of his swing while it was at its peak, and landed on his feet. "Whoa! When did you learn to do that?" Ziggy ran over to the slide and clambered up it.

Julia came out and gave Gil a hug. "What's up, Grampy?"

"I retired this week."

"Holy moly, that's great! She thought for a few seconds and said, "Wow! Are you moving to Florida?"

Gil chuckled. "No, but I might go south in the winter. Your mother never wanted to go there, but I might. It's been over a year since she died, you know, so I think it's time for me to change things up a bit. I'm going fly fishing later."

"What do you know about fly fishing?" Mike asked.

"Well, I've been watching a lot of YouTube about it, and I ordered a bunch of stuff online. I'll decide if I need some casting lessons."

Gil was glad he found a spot to park near the river where there were no other people around. He donned his chest waders and boots, put on his safety belt, chest pack, sunglasses, and hat, and hung a net off the left side of his vest. After approaching the river bank, he assembled his rod. He was ready.

He eyed a path from the river bank to a shallow, gravelly area in the middle of the stream. As he eased into the water, his leg sunk into the silt and just kept sinking. When his foot stopped sinking about two feet down, he stood awkwardly with his other foot high up on the bank. He tried to turn around to right himself, but his submerged foot was stuck in place. He threw his rod onto the bank.

There was a root sticking out of the river bank, so Gil hooked the heel of his free foot on it. This position was even more awkward, but he had enough leverage to slowly pull his mud-suctioned leg free. Relieved, he found himself sitting on dry land.

He found a better path out to the gravelly area and was getting the hang of casting his Adams dry fly. It was a beautiful afternoon, and he'd seen a couple of fish rise to the surface. After a few more casts, he heard a fish make a big splash on the surface within casting distance. Gil flicked the rod back gracefully and waited a few seconds for the fly line to stretch out behind him. He then pushed the rod forward to fling the fly toward the fish. The rod stopped mid-fling, pulling Gil so far off balance he nearly fell over. He found the culprit: his fly had caught a tree branch above the water. Damn!

He reeled in the slack and tried to pull the fly out of the tree, but it wasn't cooperating. As he continued to try, his frustration mounted. Then he heard voices. A canoe was coming around the bend. With an audience to his blunder, Gil felt himself flush with embarrassment. But the canoe passengers weren't alone. Soon, a flotilla of half a dozen canoes and kayaks floated downstream, trying their best to avoid hitting Gil, who was standing in the middle of the river with his fly in a tree. It reminded him of the time he wet his pants during recess in kindergarten, right in front of everyone on the playground. When the flotilla finally disappeared around the next bend, a fish jumped.

FOUR

The waiting room at Dr. Lipton's office was on the first floor of a Victorian mansion with a depressing collection of antique furniture and ornate pieces of art. Gil fidgeted on an uncomfortable settee while the receptionist, a masked young man named Isaac, dutifully ignored him. A coffee table offered an assortment of magazines, including back issues of *People*, *Time*, and *Saratoga Living*. Gil looked with confusion at *People* magazine where the articles were almost exclusively about celebrities he'd never heard of. Thankfully, Isaac magically appeared before him and ushered him into Dr. Lipton's office.

Craig Lipton appeared to be in his early thirties and was fit. He wore khaki slacks and a blue oxford shirt with the sleeves rolled up. He had a big flop of brown hair and wore a black cloth mask that looked too big. His hand indicated the seat Gil should take. "Glad to meet you, Mr. Novak. Please call me Craig. May I call you Gil?"

"Sure." They sat.

"I understand that you have pretty severe insomnia, and you're having nightmares that impact your sleep. Let's talk about your insomnia in general. How does your sleep go, typically?"

Gil appreciated that Craig got right into it and that they weren't starting with any fluffy stuff. "Well, I usually struggle to stay awake through the evening, nodding off occasionally. Then I go to sleep around eleven o'clock, and I usually fall asleep easily. I sleep very lightly and wake many times each night, sometimes from nightmares. At some point in the early morning, I've had enough of trying to sleep, and I get up feeling very tired. I figure I usually get two or three hours of actual sleep."

"Do you fall asleep during the day?"

"Before I retired a couple of weeks ago, I was sometimes falling asleep at work. I usually do okay in the morning, but I avoid driving in the afternoon and evening. I used to have my wife drive whenever I was feeling sleepy, but she died a year ago." His breath caught for a second. "COVID."

Gil's mind flashed back to the agony of having Cynthia unconscious in the hospital, on a ventilator, alone. The nurses had held up a tablet so Gil could talk to her for a few minutes a few times a day; it was too dangerous for him to be in the hospital with her. If she'd lived just a few more months, she could have had a vaccine.

"Oh, I'm so sorry. What was your wife's name?" Gil thought it was thoughtful that he asked.

"Cynthia." Craig was writing notes on a tablet with a stylus while they spoke.

"How long have you struggled with insomnia?"

"My whole adult life, but it's gotten much worse over the past ten years or so."

"Did you sleep okay as a child?"

"I don't really remember, but I think so."

"Please tell me about your nightmares."

Gil said, "They vary, but they have repeating elements. I often see a woman or many women breastfeeding babies. Sometimes there's a cave. A lot of times there's a monster, a wild animal like a tiger or leopard, an angel, or a devil. Sometimes

I'm being shot at. Sometimes I'm running, falling, and bleeding."

Craig took a lot of notes. "It sounds a lot like Harry Potter. Do you feel your nightmares are sexual in any way?"

"No, not at all." Gil was a little embarrassed that he knew nothing about Harry Potter.

"Have you ever had hypnotherapy?"

"No, I've never been hypnotized."

"I think it would be a good idea to try and get rid of your nightmares with hypnotherapy. This would allow us to explore your nightmares and put them into perspective. Would you be open to using hypnotherapy for this?"

"I'm open to hypnosis as long as you don't make me think I'm a chicken."

Craig laughed. "I promise not to make you a chicken. I'll schedule you for two one-hour appointments. I'll record the sessions so we can go back and listen to them, if we need to. Afterward, we'll schedule a follow-up session, and we can see how effective we were at getting the nightmares to stop, or at least turning them from nightmares into dreams that don't impact your sleep."

FIVE

The young mother was sitting on the ground in the leaves, breastfeeding her baby. As Gil watched, he felt as serene and joyful as if he were that baby. Suddenly a piercing screech filled the air, a sound so loud and horrible it knocked the wind out of him. The mother's face jerked up with fear, and her baby started to wail. Another long screech tore through his ears, and a horrible monster, like a hyena with no fur, crawled steadily toward the mother. The mother set her baby in the leaves as she stood up, shaking her fist with anger. "No, no!" she yelled, but the monster approached.

Gil snapped up to a sitting position as he awoke, shaking, sweating, and breathing heavily as the morning sun leaked in through gaps in the curtains. Another day.

After his cup of decaf, Gil read the online news on his laptop, then mowed the lawn. One yogurt later, he changed into his new bicycling outfit: black spandex shorts and a chartreuse short-sleeved shirt, both of which were a bit too tight around the waist. The shorts had gel cushions for his crotch, which felt peculiar. He filled his water bottle, pumped up his tires, put on his helmet and sunglasses, then headed out on his seldom-used bicycle. It was a beautiful, early-summer day, heavy with the smell of plant life. His route was more forests than fields, and so he hit pockets of warmer and cooler air as he rode along, which he found pleasurable. Often the heavy scent of flowers lingered in his nose for a while.

He rode up a gradual, mile-long hill, and he felt great doing it, raising his confidence. He rode by a horse farm where a few young foals chased each other around the older grazing horses. He rode through a hatch of gnats, trying not to breathe them in. Riding seemed almost effortless. He thought about Amelia working remotely and living her West Coast, COVID-hampered lifestyle. She had told him that she was "hanging out" with a guy, so maybe that meant she had a love interest. Gil wanted to go visit her, but he wasn't quite ready to fly during the pandemic. Maybe he would drive out there. Maybe on a motorcycle!

Gil woke up with a start as his shoulder hit the grass. He slid a few feet into a drainage ditch. He stayed still for a moment to sense if he was injured. A few aches, but nothing deep. He felt mostly okay. He slowly stood up, getting scratched by a pricker bush that caught him. Shit. He picked up his bike, which seemed to be okay. Very lucky. Had anybody ever fallen asleep while riding a bike?

The right side of his spandex shorts had split almost all the way up, except for the waistband and bottom hem. His modesty in jeopardy, he had to do something. He took a drink from his water bottle while he considered his options, and he casually swung around to conceal his embarrassment as a car drove by. He removed a shoelace from his right shoe and attempted to use it to stitch up the hole. Surprisingly, it worked pretty well, but he wasn't sure how long it would last. He got back on his bike and pedaled carefully so as not to pull out the stitches or lose the sneaker missing its shoelace.

SIX

The monster screeched hideously as the angel floated above it, blocking its path. Whichever way the monster turned, the angel did also, her spectral white gown a barrier the monster could not pass. The monster whipped around once more, suddenly face-to-face with a burgundy-colored devil. It had evil eyes and carried a pitchfork. The monster screeched as it lunged at the devil, who snatched the monster out of the air and effortlessly flung it away. The devil confronted the angel, but she hovered around him and laughed. But the devil's attention was elsewhere. It sniffed the air, turned toward Gil, and pointed.

Gil woke up nervous and sweating. He sat up and felt sore all over from his bike ride. He would need a recovery day.

————————

After puttering around the house doing minor chores, Gil took an afternoon nap in preparation for his monthly poker game. Reggie would host tonight. Gil parked his car on the grass circle in the middle of Reggie's cul-de-sac. He knocked and let himself in, finding Reggie talking to Mike in the kitchen. Gil said hi and went out to the screened-in deck, where he set his bag of quarters on the table. They chatted and nibbled on some hors d'oeuvres as the others arrived.

Seven players were at the table—the optimal number for their poker games. It was Gil's deal, so he announced, "Seven card, high-low, they are what they are." He put in the ante for the whole table, as was their custom, and he dealt everybody the first two cards down and the third card up. Everybody plunked quarters into the pot in turn, and Gil dealt the next cards up. As he dealt the sixth card to everybody, he reminded them that the next two bets would be fifty cents instead of a quarter.

Everyone could tell by then, based on the showing cards, who likely had good high hands and good low hands. Omar and Brad had already folded. Gil had a pair of tens and a pair of eights, which was a weak high hand, but he stayed in, hoping for a miracle. Quarters plunked in. Gil dealt the last card down. Gil still only had two pairs, but he decided to stay in. Nobody else folded.

"Final bets," Gil said. The betting went around the table a couple of times, with Geordie and Reggie raising. "Okay, what do we have?"

Mike said, "Three sixes."

Geordie said, "Perfect low."

Reggie said, "I also got a perfect."

Turner said, "I have three threes—but I also have two jacks!" Mike threw down his cards in disgust.

"Just two pair," Gil said. "Okay, you two split the low, and Turner gets the high." They went about splitting the pot while Gil passed the deck to Omar.

Each dealer chose different versions of poker. They played Hold'em, Ten Pack, the Whole Enchilada, Omaha, and so forth. Halfway through the evening, they took a snack break and gathered around the kitchen island.

Nick, who was good at picking up bluffs, eyed Gil. "What's with the club soda?"

"I'm on a health kick, now that I've retired."

Everybody stopped talking.

Geordie said, "What? When did you retire?"

"Two weeks ago." They gathered around, offering congratulations, and asking about his plans.

An hour later, a shudder went through Gil, and he realized his head was on the table. He opened his eyes and sat up, quickly wiping the stream of drool between the corner of his mouth and his hand. Everybody had smirks on their faces. Gil looked at his quarters: there were only two left. "What happened?"

"You must have been sleep-betting," Reggie said. "You had really lousy hands, but you kept throwing quarters into the pot!" They all burst out laughing. Turner dumped his quarters back in front of him and slapped him on the back.

"Gil, seriously?" Mike said. "Falling asleep in the middle of poker?"

"I'm sorry. I've got a serious insomnia problem, and I just started seeing a neurologist. It's really bad. It's one of the reasons I retired."

Mike offered a thoughtful look. "Well, I hope they can help you with that. Insomnia can be pretty serious."

He didn't tell them about his bike incident.

SEVEN

Isaac, the receptionist, wore a cloth mask with a picture of cherries on it. He ushered Gil into Dr. Lipton's office for Gil's first hypnosis session. "Hi, Gil. Have a seat over here, and we'll get to know each other a little better. It'll help you to relax, plus I'm generally nosy about people. I'll start. I'm a psychotherapist, and I've been in practice for eleven years. I'm originally from New York City and went to school there, but my family used to come up here to see the horse races when I was a kid, so I decided to move here after school. How about you? Are you from Saratoga originally?"

"Actually, I grew up in a small town called Greenfield, Massachusetts, which is near Brattleboro, Vermont. I went to college at UMass for engineering, and I got hired at Adirondack Robotics right out of school."

"Very cool! Tell me about your family."

"As I told you last time, my wife Cynthia died last year from COVID."

"Yes, I'm so sorry."

"I have two daughters, a son-in-law, and three grandkids. My older daughter, her husband, and their kids live here in Saratoga. My single daughter lives in California."

"What are your hobbies, what do you like to do with your free time?"

"Well, I used to spend my time buying and renovating houses for resale, but I think I've had enough of that. I've been trying new hobbies lately, like fly fishing and bike riding. I read a lot of novels, and I love to go to the movies, but I guess I haven't been since COVID hit. I hope to travel more when COVID goes away."

"Yeah, COVID isn't helping, is it? Well, any changes to your sleep problem?"

"No, it's still a big problem. Maybe worse. Believe it or not, I fell asleep while taking a bike ride."

Craig's jaw dropped. "Really? That's a new one on me. You may be transitioning into narcolepsy." He wrote that down. "You may have to stop driving. When's your next appointment with Dr. Manomoney?

"Not for a while."

"I'll have her set something up to discuss this change. Do you have any idea when your nightmares started or what may have caused them?"

"I have no idea, but I bet it would help my insomnia if you could help me get rid of them."

"Well, I think I can help you with that. I've had quite a bit of success helping people to get rid of their nightmares. Nightmares are a fairly common problem. Would you describe them for me in more detail? Are they always the same?"

"There are several different versions, and they repeat. Some parts of them are pleasant, and some cause me a lot of stress."

"Tell me about the pleasant parts."

"Well, it's a little embarrassing."

"Don't worry. Dreams can seem embarrassing to talk about, but talking about them is what will help them stop. Of course, nobody but you and I will discuss your dreams."

"Well, one pleasant part involves a lot of breasts. Sometimes I see a sea of breasts with or without women, and sometimes I see a single girl with her shirt off. I usually see a baby or many babies feeding from these breasts. The thing is, I never feel sexually aroused by these breasts. I just get this pleasant, comfortable feeling." Craig was taking notes. "Another pleasant thing is this angel. She is dressed in shimmering and flowing white, and she's floating above the ground. Sometimes she protects the girl with the breasts and her baby."

"Do you know these girls?"

"No, but I can't quite tell what their faces look like."

"Do you recognize any of the babies?"

This question surprised him. "I don't think so. I don't think I ever tried to recognize the babies."

"Any other pleasant things in your dreams?"

"Sometimes I'm in a forest, and I can smell the trees and leaves."

"Okay, please try and describe the stressful parts of your dreams."

"The worst one is when I'm being shot at, and bullets are hitting the ground all around me. Another one is when I'm tripping and falling on rocks, usually trying to escape the bullets. Sometimes there's a monster that screeches horribly and tries to attack the girl who is breastfeeding. And sometimes there's a devil who comes after me." Gil felt uncomfortable and looked away.

"I can see that you get stressed out just remembering these things. Today I'll introduce you to hypnosis, and we'll only investigate the pleasant parts of your dreams. Sound good?" Gil nodded. "We'll use hypnosis to help you observe your nightmares objectively and without anxiety. When you become relaxed while having these dreams, they won't be nightmares anymore. It's unlikely that we'll learn much about why they started. Hypnosis isn't really a tool for retrieving memories. It's more about relaxation."

"First, let's start with some relaxation techniques." Gil noticed immediately that Craig was talking in a slower, smoother voice. "Close your eyes. Now take a deep breath, and let it out slowly. Now do another cleansing breath, even slower. Good, we'll have you relax deeply, working your way from the top of your head down. Each time you breathe out, relax all the muscles in your head and face and let them go slack: your scalp, your eyes, your ears, your mouth, your chin. Good. Now relax the muscles in your neck and your shoulders. Relax your upper arms, lower arms, and hands, all the way to your fingertips. Good. Now relax your chest and let your stomach and back muscles go slack. Good. Now relax your pelvic area, then your thighs, your knees, your calves, and your feet, all the way to the tips of your toes.

"Good. Now imagine that a cloud of deep warmth is falling into the top of your head, filling your head and face, down through your neck and chest, through your arms, hands, and fingers, filling your chest, your stomach, spreading down into your pelvis, your thighs, calves, feet, and all the way through the tips of your toes and continuing to flow out of your feet and toes. This cloud is full of warmth and pleasure. How does this make you feel?"

Gil thought about it and said, "I feel very relaxed and comfortable, like I'm in a Jacuzzi."

"Good. Now imagine you're at the top of a stairway that goes to a wonderful place. How would you describe this stairway?"

"It's an escalator. A new, clean escalator that's colored like a nickel alloy with black plastic moving handrails. The stairs are grooved toward the direction of travel, and they're moving downward, like any typical escalator."

"Good. Next, you're going to descend the escalator as I count down from ten, and each time I count, you're going to feel more and more relaxed. Now step onto the escalator. Ten, you're feeling more relaxed. Nine, now even more. Eight. Seven. Six. You can see that the lighting is very dim at the bottom. Five. Four. Three. Two. And one. Step off the escalator and tell me how you feel."

"I feel very, very relaxed. I want to know where I am."

"Your eyes are adjusting to the dim lighting, and you can see that you're in a small movie theater, all alone. Imagine that you are taking a seat in this theater, and we'll start the movie soon. Where are you sitting?

"I'm sitting in a middle row, to the right of the center aisle."

"Are you relaxed and comfortable?"

"I'm very relaxed and comfortable."

"Good. Now we'll start the movie. You have a remote in your hand, and you can control this movie, so you can start it and pause it whenever you like. You also control what you'll be seeing. You'll be watching parts of your recurring dreams. Do you understand?"

"Yes, I understand."

"Good. Now press the play button, and let's watch the first time you saw a young woman breastfeeding her baby in your dreams." Gil imagined he had a remote in his hand and pressed the play button. Craig said, "Now describe the scene to me as it plays."

"I'm lying prone in a pile of leaves, hiding behind a rocky knoll. I see a girl who's sitting on a big log next to a large outcropping of red igneous rock. She's wearing farmer-style blue-jean overalls, but her shirt is completely off, and the bib of her overalls is down, exposing her breasts. She has a baby suckling her left breast. The air smells fresh, and it's warm and sunny out, like spring."

"Tell me where you are," Craig said.

"I'm at Poet's Seat Mountain, on the far side."

"How old are you?" Craig asked.

The image on the movie screen showed Gil's perspective, and he could look down at his arms and his clothes. "I'm about fourteen. The girl is only about sixteen, I think. Wait, I hear someone else."

"Press pause now," Craig said. "Do you know this girl? Do you know her name?"

"No."

"How does it make you feel, seeing this young woman breastfeeding her baby?"

"I feel wonderful, almost like I was that baby."

"Good," Craig said. "Now fast-forward to the first time you saw the angel."

"I have to rewind because it's before." Gil rewound and then pressed play. "I'm in the same spot, but with a friend. The young mother is there holding her baby with her shirt on. There are two men and a woman talking. Hippies. The angel emerges from a cleft in the rocks."

"Tell me what the people are saying."

"I can't hear the words, but sometimes they laugh."

"Describe the angel."

"She's a girl that's eleven or twelve. She's floating above the ground wearing a white, translucent dress. Her dress and hair are flowing with the breeze. She has dark hair with white flowers in it."

"Now press the pause button. How do you feel?"

"I feel exhilaration and amazement."

"Who is the friend with you?"

"Micky."

"You're doing great, Gil. Now I'd like you to go to the up-going escalator. When you step onto the escalator, I'll count to ten, and as I do, you'll feel more and more rested, and your mind will feel clearer. You will remember what you observed in the movie. When you reach the top, you will become fully awake and alert. Now step onto the escalator. One, you are feeling rested, and your mind is getting clearer. Two, three, four, five, six, seven, eight, nine, ten! You step off the top of the escalator, and you're now fully awake and alert."

Gil opened his eyes.

"How do you feel?"

"I feel great. But I'm confused about what I saw. They were my dreams, but they didn't feel the same."

"We've removed the anxiety that you've felt when you see these dreams. In your nightmares, even the positive parts are connected with anxiety. Do you remember the place where these dreams are, this Poet's Seat Mountain?"

"Sure. Me and my friends used to hang around up there. I can sort of remember finding a cave up there with Micky

Tindall. Wow, I haven't seen him in decades. Maybe I'll track him down and see if we can find it."

Craig was still taking notes. "Well, Gil, today we initiated hypnotherapy, and I think it was extremely successful. You're very receptive to it. Next time, it'll be even easier to initiate hypnosis and get you back into your movie theater. By the way, you're the first of my patients that's ever envisioned an escalator, and I think that's very cool. Next time we'll carefully explore some of the more difficult aspects of your dreams. But I like your plan. I think it would be good if you connect with Micky, talk with him about what happened, and find that cave. What do you think? Any questions?"

"Well, I was relaxed during hypnosis, but will this relaxation be long term?"

"After our next session, when we explore the more stressful parts of your nightmares in the relaxed hypnotic state, you won't tie them to feelings of anxiety later on. They won't be nightmares anymore. I'll also teach you how to perform relaxation exercises by yourself and how to use that capability in the future."

EIGHT

The young mother was sitting on a log, feeding her baby by a cave entrance. Under a bright-blue tarp canopy, she was safe from the sun, except for the sliver of light cutting the back of her hair. Suddenly, a shrill scream pierced the air. A snarling beast kicked up leaves and dust as it approached her. She yelled at the beast, but it kept coming. A younger girl came running out of the cave and got in front of the beast, waving her arms and yelling. Then the beast leaped upon her, ripping and tearing.

Gil sat up in bed, drenched in sweat, trying to catch his breath. The clock said 4:55 a.m. He turned on the light and wrote down what had happened in his sleep log. After rinsing his face in the bathroom, he turned on a small table lamp in the living room, sat in his reclining chair, and read the novel he'd recently started on his Kindle. Gil always had a book in progress, usually fiction. After about twenty minutes, he shut off the light and went back to bed. More sleep was not forthcoming, so his day started in earnest just before six.

———

Gil drove to the pickleball courts at Gavin Park just after eight o'clock, hoping to arrange a lesson before the crowd arrived. He'd bought a paddle online. A woman dressed in tennis attire was setting out bins of pink wiffle balls.

"Excuse me, I'm looking for a pickleball lesson. My name is Gil."

She sized him up for a second. "I'll be done setting up in a couple of minutes, then I'll give you a lesson. My name is Marion." When she was done she came over and asked, "Do you know anything about pickleball?"

"Well, I read about it online and watched a few YouTube videos."

"Good, that's more than a lot of people do. Here, let's go close to the net and just start hitting the ball." Gil found it pretty easy to hit the ball after a bounce or in the air. As they continued, Marion explained the rules of the game, which Gil found a little confusing.

"Okay, over here is the kitchen," Gil confirmed, "and I can't go in there except for when?"

"If somebody hits a dink shot, which is a very short shot, and it lands in the kitchen, you can step into the kitchen to hit the ball. But then you have to get right out of there for your next hit."

"I think I got it, but the scoring still confuses me."

Marion smiled. "By the end of the day, you'll get it. It's simple: score and know whether you're the first or second server in that round. Like five–two–two means it's five to two, your team is leading, and you're the second server, which means that once you lose a point, the serve goes to the other team. Let's have you practice a few serves." Marion explained how to serve and return serves, which seemed pretty straightforward. Other players started to arrive and warm up. After a couple of more minutes, Marion said, "Wait right here a minute." She went to the next court and spoke to the players and brought a couple back with her. "This is Jim and Joanie. They agreed to help teach you how to play, so let's get started."

They got right into it, and Gil was able to play. He made a lot of mistakes and felt clumsy, but he gained confidence as they played, especially after making a few great shots. Marion and Gil lost the game eleven to six, but Gil was happy with that. Marion brought him over to the bench and told him to stack his paddle onto the paddle pile. As people's turns came up, they pulled their paddles from the bottom of the pile to go play. Gil drank from his water bottle, watched others play, chatted with other waiting players, and played another two games. Gil thanked Marion and told her that he planned to play regularly.

NINE

It was a beautiful morning when Gil parked his car at the Kayak Shak on Fish Creek. A couple of college-aged girls were enthusiastically running the place that day, and they got him set up to paddle. As he got ready to shove off, he asked, "Should I go right or left?"

The girl said, "You can't go very far to the right because it gets shallow, so left is better. But you can do both!" And she gave him a big shove into the water. Gil headed left, against the current. The creek flowed east toward the Hudson River, but the water moved so slowly that Gil hardly noticed any drag. The paddling was easy, and he saw a lot of ducks, a great blue heron, and some jumping fish. Eventually, he paddled around a big bend, and the creek widened as it headed past the big rowing center. Little motor boats trailed fully teamed rowing shells of different sizes. Some shells had coxswains keeping pace by yelling into loudspeakers. Most of the boats had kids rowing, but a few had adults. Maybe Gil would try rowing.

He paddled under the Route 9P bridge, then through the headwaters of the creek and into Saratoga Lake. The lake water was choppy, jostling Gil around in his kayak, so he decided to head back. He negotiated a few waves as he turned around and found himself heading into a steady wind. Now it took a lot more effort to make headway. Water splashed over the bow, getting Gil wet. His hat flew off his head, but when he turned around to grab it, it had already disappeared. With great effort, he paddled to the far to the right side of the creek to stay out of the way of the rowing shells. The wind was calmer near that shore, it seemed, and he eventually made it to the big bend in the creek, where the wind and waves subsided. He was soaking wet, but it felt good in the heat. He drank from his water bottle to stay hydrated and paddled back to the Kayak Shak.

———————

"Thanks for having me for dinner," said Gil. The younger kids, Ziggy and Dez, were seated on either side of him, their food cut up into tiny pieces. Jazz was sitting in the corner, looking at her cell phone. Gil asked, "Ziggy, when are you going to learn to cut up your own food?"

He blushed and stared at his mom. "Maybe since he's six now, he can learn," Julia said. "Jazz, put your phone down. So, Grampy, what have you been up to?"

"I've been trying different hobbies. I went fly fishing on the Battenkill River, I went on a long bike ride, I played pickleball, and this morning, I went kayaking over on Fish Creek."

Ziggy asked, "What's pickleball?"

"It's a cross between tennis and ping-pong. You play on a very small tennis court using paddles that are a little bigger than ping-pong paddles. The ball is a pink wiffle ball. It's fun!"

"Wow, you're doing a lot!" said Mike. "What else are you going to try?"

"I'm thinking about belly dancing."

Jazz and Dez burst out laughing. Ziggy looked distraught.

"Grampy's just kidding," said Julia. "He's not going to be belly dancing, I hope." More giggling. "How's your sleeping?"

"It's still horrible, but I've started therapy for it. I got hypnotized!"

"Wow! What was that like?" asked Julia.

"It's hard to describe. The therapist talked me through relaxation techniques, and I was in a super-relaxed state of some sort. He then asked me to remember certain aspects of my nightmares so I could remember them without being stressed."

"Is it working?"

"Not yet, but I've only just started. Right now, I'm limited to driving in the morning, but I'm optimistic. I think getting more active and losing some weight will help too. I think I'm going to make myself a cup of decaf. Does anybody else want coffee? Dez, you want a cup of coffee?" Dez giggled and shook her head with an emphatic no.

Gil sat in an Adirondack chair on the front porch drinking his decaf. Ziggy and Dez were drawing with chalk on the driveway. After a few minutes, Julia sat down next to him, and Gil's eyes cracked open.

"Oh, did I wake you?" Julia asked. "I'm so sorry. I think it's great that you've launched into trying all these hobbies. So far, pickleball is the only one involving other people though."

"Yeah, I know. It's probably time I try for some more socialization."

"When are you going to take your ring off?"

Gil looked at it, twirled it around a bit, and decided to take it off right then and there. He pulled, but it wasn't going to come off. "Can you get me some dental floss?" Julia looked at him curiously. She brought him a container of floss, and Gil wound a long piece tightly around his knuckle and through the ring. He slowly unwound the floss and it smoothly moved the ring over his knuckle and off. "There. It's off." Gil stuck it in his pocket.

TEN

Dr. Lipton said, "Okay, now you're sitting in the theater with the remote in your hand. How are you feeling?"

Gil's eyes were closed. "I'm very relaxed."

Craig continued, "Remember, you control the remote, and you can pause it at any time. Now we're going to watch the last time you saw the angel. Go ahead, press play, and tell me what you see."

"The young mother is breastfeeding her baby just outside of the cave entrance," Gil said calmly. "I hear a horrible screech, and then I see this creature crawling out of the trees toward her."

"Describe this creature," said Craig.

"Oh, now I see that it's not a creature. It's a small child, but it's deformed. Very deformed. Its spine is twisted, and its head and face are misshapen—kind of like an asymmetrical football with patchy hair. Its eyes are too wide apart, and they're not level. One of its legs is too long, and it's screeching, awfully. I think it's about three years old."

"Describe what happens next."

"The young mother yells at the child, but I can't hear what she says. I think she's telling it to go away. It keeps coming and screeching. The angel comes out of the cave, floating in the air, and she gets between the mother and the deformed child. The child turns around and crawls farther into the woods, grunting as it moves." Gil suddenly spoke more urgently. "I feel thuds in the ground next to me and smell the dirt. I hear cracks in the air. Someone is shooting at me."

"Press pause," said Craig. "Now take some deep, slow breaths in and out. Relax." Gil breathed deeply for a little while to get more relaxed. "Remember, you can push the pause button at any time. You are in control. You don't need to worry about the shooting because you are here now, and you're okay. You're just watching your dream on the movie screen. How do you feel?"

"I'm relaxing. But I could use another minute." His breathing slowed.

"Look around and tell me who is shooting at you."

"I can't see who is shooting."

"Okay, push the slow-motion button on the remote." Gil lifted the imaginary remote, which seemed to have a real weight to it, and pushed a button. "Now press play and describe what happens."

"The mother's head comes up, and she looks down the mountain. I look over there, but I don't see anyone. I turn around and take off in slow motion while trying to crouch down. I hear a few more bullets kicking up dirt around my feet. I try to run faster, but the loose rocks, sticks, and leaves are slippery. I slip and fall slowly to the ground. I hit my head on some rocks. I see stars, and I can't move. I'm afraid I'm going to be shot and killed, but I can't move." Gil remains relaxed.

"Go on," Craig said.

"The video is frozen now."

"Okay, you've gone as far as you can go," Craig said. "Now go over to the escalator and go back up. By the time I count to ten, you'll be fully awake, feel fully rested, and remember everything you saw in the movie."

Once Gil was fully awake with his eyes open, Craig asked, "How do you feel?"

"I feel fine. I'm intrigued! On one hand, the mystery of the monster has been cleared up, I think. On the other hand, it seems like someone was really shooting at me, and I did fall and maybe lost consciousness."

"Well, remember that the things you saw or think you clarified aren't necessarily true at all." Craig set down his notebook. "Dreams are not reflective of our memories. Also, as we've discussed, hypnosis can't magically cause you to remember exactly what happened in the past. Memories get corrupted over time. There are studies showing that memories get a little more corrupted each time they are remembered. Since you've been dredging up memories in your nightmares all these years, your memories may be very corrupted. The most we could say is that there may be some correlation between what you saw today and what actually happened. Remember, our intent is to allow you to observe your dreams in a relaxed state so they don't produce anxiety."

"Well, we did that, so maybe with some cognitive behavioral therapy from Dr. Manomoney, I can get to sleeping normally."

"Do you remember what happened when you went home with an injured head?"

"I have no idea. I'm guessing that I would have tried to hide it from my mother. That part doesn't give me any nightmares though."

"Is your mother still with us?"

"No, she died a few years ago," said Gil.

35

"I'm very sorry about that." He paused respectfully and picked up his notes. "In our last session, you described these people as hippies, like they're a distinct type of people. How would you describe hippies as opposed to people who aren't hippies?"

Gil laughed. "I'm sorry, I took it for granted that you'd know about hippies, but it was way before your time. The hippies dressed in a certain way, the girls with long, decorated skirts, bell-bottom jeans, or cut-off jean short shorts. The guys had bell-bottomed jeans and suede jackets or army jackets, and everybody wore lots of beads and had long or big, bushy hair. The guys had beards. There were a lot of hippies and communes in the area of New England where I grew up."

Craig smiled and said, "I guess I had a similar picture in my mind when you mentioned them, but I've really never read anything about them. I'll have to learn more. Anyway, I'd say we accomplished what we needed to, for now. As you go further with Prisha's CBTI therapy, please give me a call if you need another session."

ELEVEN

Maybe Gil's daughters would think he was enjoying being single too much, or maybe he'd end up inspiring them. Whatever the case, Gil had decided to do whatever he felt like doing for a while, and that meant buying a motorcycle. For a couple of months, he'd looked longingly at a bike in the showroom window of a Ford dealer that he often drove by. A couple of days ago, he stopped and bought it. It was a beautiful blue BMW touring bike with all the bells and whistles, and it only had about two thousand miles on it. It had been over thirty years since he last owned a motorcycle.

He packed for a couple of nights and headed toward Greenfield. While riding his motorcycle, Gil felt excitement combined with unbridled joy. He was a careful rider, no longer captivated by the adolescent need for speed. After riding slowly and steadily across the metal-grate bridge over the Hudson River, he rolled through the countryside of eastern New York, inundated by intoxicating bursts of perfume coming from flowering plants. In Vermont, he took the bypass road around Bennington, then he headed up into the Green Mountains. The air got a little cooler as he gained altitude, but after reaching the summit, he descended into hot and humid air. He loved feeling closer to nature.

At the bottom of the mountains, the water in the Deerfield River wasn't low like it usually was in summer. There had been quite a lot of rain over the past few weeks. He cruised by Dot's Restaurant in Wilmington, where his family had experienced many great breakfasts when the kids were young. He headed down winding Route 100 into Jacksonville and then turned south toward Massachusetts. After passing through "downtown" Colrain, he was happy to find the bumpy back road into Greenfield open. It suffered some kind of damage every winter, and getting repair money often took a couple of years. That day, it was newly paved and smooth.

In Greenfield, Gil pulled into the parking lot at Denny's Pantry. As he took off his helmet and jacket in his hometown, he felt nostalgic but also plagued by the shadow of depression he unjustly acquired while growing up there. As a child, he felt that his life was excruciatingly boring, and it seemed like forever until he could finally move out and go to college. He assumed millions of teenage kids everywhere in the world felt that way. Taking a seat at a small table outside under a tent, he ordered a tuna melt sandwich and looked around to see if he recognized anyone. He didn't.

After lunch, he rode up to Poet's Seat Tower, a red sandstone structure with a beautiful view overlooking the town and surrounding countryside. According to the brass plaque, the tower was built in the early 1900s in honor of Frederick Goddard Tuckerman, a gifted local poet of some renown during the mid-1800s. He realized that he'd never read any of Tuckerman's poems, so he made a mental note to google Tuckerman. Gil stowed his helmet and jacket in the top box on his bike, then climbed up the tower stairs.

The 360-degree view was a little hazy but still beautiful. He picked out his old neighborhood and other familiar sites, but the town's huge leafy trees limited what he could see. He remembered climbing up the cliff face with his childhood friends. There were two climbable clefts in the cliff below the tower called the lemon squeeze and the orange squeeze. He wondered who had named those clefts.

When he'd had enough of reminiscing, he set out to find the cave of his nightmares. All he could remember was that it lay on the side of the mountain opposite the town, which headed down to the western bank of the Connecticut River. He walked slowly down the hill, trying to avoid losing his footing on the loose rocks, leaves, and sticks. For the past couple of years, he sometimes experienced this strange feeling that his mind wasn't always fully synchronized with his body. He was less confident in his balance, and sometimes he even momentarily lost track of where he was and where he was headed. Gil hoped these weren't early signs of dementia. If he did get injured, though, at least he could call for help on his cell phone. He didn't have that safety measure when he was up there as a child.

He got most of the way down and could see the river through the trees, but there was no sign of rocky areas that could hide a cave. The river was a grayish-brown color, which was much better than the bright metallic green of his childhood. The upstream factories that polluted the water had long since been closed. He trudged back uphill at an angle toward the north, and he eventually encountered some promising rock formations. Still no caves. He headed back toward his bike, having decided to get some help.

He backed his bike into one of the angled parking spots on Main Street. The parking meter only accepted coins, so he popped into a store to get change for a dollar. He put some quarters in the parking meter and took a walk. Wilson's department store, the hub of downtown for his entire childhood, had recently gone out of business and sat empty. Plenty of other little shops and restaurants had kept the town surviving with some optimism, but all of these businesses were different from the ones that Gil knew growing up. His family moved away soon after he started college, and he hadn't been back more than a few times.

He got back on his bike and rode through his old neighborhood. Not much had changed. Lots of well-kept, modest houses with trees all around. His elementary school buildings had been repurposed. His high school had been expanded, but it still had the institutional look of a school building. He rode out to the country club, parked, and put on his mask. At the club restaurant, one of the servers brought him to a table on the veranda, where he sat down and de-masked. His table overlooked the golf course, which appeared to be in peak condition. A few groups of golfers were on the course playing the game, all dressed in shorts and polo shirts.

Micky strode in. Gil hadn't seen him in over twenty years, but he recognized him right away. Same guy, with more weight and less hair. Micky was wearing a dark-gray suit, medium-blue shirt, and no necktie. He looked around, and Gil gave him a wave. "Gil!" Micky said when he noticed and gave his old friend an elbow bump. He took off his jacket and draped it over an adjacent chair before removing his mask and sitting down. "It's great to see you after all these years. What have you been up to? I remember that you're an engineer of some sort."

"Well, now I'm a retired engineer. I worked on designing and building manufacturing-line robots in Saratoga Springs. I just retired a couple of weeks ago, so now I'm trying to decide whether to be a geezer or a curmudgeon." Micky laughed. "How about you? Are you still lawyering?"

"Yeah. For a long time, I was partner in a corporate law firm in Springfield, but a few years back I decided to slow down, so I hung out my shingle in Greenfield as a general-purpose lawyer. I've mostly been doing family law, but I have some small-business work too."

Our server introduced herself as Justy and took their drink orders: beer for Micky and lemonade for Gil.

Suddenly, a booming voice from right behind Gil said, "Ah, the illustrious Gil Novak, one of the many who reached escape velocity to seek planets beyond our lovely hometown. Hi, Mick."

It was Eddie Locke, the smiling, bear-like man who Gil had seen at most of his high school reunions. "Hi, Eddie," said Gil. "How are you doing?"

Looking incredulous, he said, "This can't be a coincidence. Have you come to surreptitiously observe the annual mud dance?"

Gil gave him *the look*. "I'll bite. What is the annual mud dance?"

"I'm shocked that you, with your ancient ties to Greenfield, are not familiar with this most sacred of rituals. It is, of course, when a multitude of substantial, yet scantily clad, post-virginal girls wade into the mud-laden shallows of the Green River, up around the bend. They rhythmically waggle their arm waddles in hopes of ensuring a bountiful kielbasa harvest, while simultaneously keeping their toddlers from drowning."

Both Micky and Gil tried to play it cool, but they burst out laughing. Gil looked at Eddie with wonder, shrugged his shoulders, and said, "Yeah, I'm up for that. Who wouldn't want to see scantily clad, substantial girls mucking around? I must admit, Eddie, that you haven't changed a bit since high school. You still have a flair for creative prose."

"Well, a big part of my job is helping to prepare the Massachusetts state budget, which, I must admit, is quite fanciful."

"Would you like to join us for dinner?" Gil asked.

"Well I'd love to, but I have to pass. I'll shortly be meeting my lovely young friend. She requires consoling after being judged too petite for this year's mud dance. Have a great evening, gentlemen!"

Micky shook off the spectacle that was Eddie and asked, "So what's this mysterious thing you're researching? You were kind of cryptic over the phone."

As Gil was about to answer, Justy appeared with their drinks and took their dinner orders: salmon napolitano for Gil and chicken piccata for Micky. Gil asked, "Do you remember our Wrist Rocket slingshots?"

Micky looked at him quizzically, then laughed. "Sure! Remember when Larry took yours and launched a marble through the plate-glass window of McDonald's?"

Gil laughed. "I didn't remember that until you said it. In Larry's defense, though, it was completely unintentional. He just shot blindly into the air over the roof of the Carlson's house. It was a stupid thing to do, but we did a lot of stupid things back then. Anyway, do you remember climbing up Poet's Seat with those slingshots and hiking down toward the river? We stumbled upon some hippies in a cave."

Micky scrunched his nose and said, "Yeah, I kinda do remember that. We just sort of spied on 'em for a few minutes and snuck away."

"Well, I never told you this, but I went back the next day to spy on them some more." Gil went on to explain what he thought he remembered about that whole incident, including being shot at. Gil also told Micky about his struggle with insomnia and his hypnosis treatment.

Micky sat back in his chair. "Wow, that sounds like more of a fantasy than the kielbasa mud dance! So what are you trying to do?"

"I don't really know. It seems like if I make more sense of what I saw back then, my nightmares might go away. I went up to Poet's Seat this afternoon and looked around, but I couldn't find the cave."

Micky said, "Do you remember Bear's Den?"

"Sure, but—"

"I know, that cave is different and in a different area. I just wanted to make sure you knew that. Do you know the brick DPW shed on the road up to the tower? I'm not sure, but that cave might be down the mountain toward the river from that building."

Gil said, "Yeah, I remember that little brick building. I'll go up again tomorrow and take a look." Gil looked across the veranda and saw Eddie eating an appetizer with his pretty girlfriend. "I think Eddie's young lady is really about the same age as we are, but I would agree that she may be too petite for the mud dance."

TWELVE

As soon as Remi Foy got out of his rusty station wagon, he could hear screams coming out of the old hunting cabin. Drunk, he stumbled to the door and fell back on the dirt as he pulled the door open. He pulled himself back up and went in to find Marie, his thirteen-year-old daughter in labor. His wife, Jacqui, and his younger daughter, Angela, were helping.

"Stop screaming!" he slurred. "I don't want nobody comin' round here."

Jacqui squealed with laughter and said, "You aren't going to get a girl in labor to stop yellin'. Now get out of here and shut the door. This will take a couple of hours, at least. This is your fault anyway."

Remi went back to the car, grabbed his flask of whiskey, and headed to the pond. He sat on his favorite rock ledge, lit up a Kool, took a swig of whiskey, and passed out. The flask fell, spilling most of the whiskey onto the dirt. The cigarette burned a small hole in his shirt.

Remi woke with a start when a mosquito bit him on his eyelid. It was dark out, but the moon was bright. His head pounded, and his dry mouth felt like it was full of rotten meat. He found the near-empty flask and felt around for the cap so he could save what was left. A wave of nausea hit him when he stood up, but he recovered and was able to walk, tripping over the occasional tree root. When he got back to the cabin, the glow of a gas lantern snuck through the cracks around the shutters. He went in and found Marie in bed, holding a baby swaddled in a flannel shirt. Angela was sleeping on her little mattress in the corner, and Jacqui was tending a fire in the wood stove.

"Well, what is it?" Remi asked.

Jacqui said, "It's a boy, and he looks just like his daddy." She cackled.

Remi went over to Marie and reached for the baby, but she pulled it away from him. He grabbed the baby, and Marie moaned in protest.

He gasped as he pulled back the flannel. "What's this? It's a fucking freak!" He pushed it back into Marie's hands and ran out the door. He leaned against a tree, puking.

THIRTEEN

June 2021—Greenfield, Massachusetts

Gil stared at his face in the bathroom mirror, wondering if he should try for a scruffy look like some actors. After having slept deeply until about 2:30 a.m., he'd given up on forcing more restless sleep at five. Still, a little better than before he started hypnotherapy. He still woke up dreaming, but there hadn't been any nightmares lately.

Gil defaulted to his regular clean-shaven look, thinking more gray hair would just make him look older. He made a cup of decaf with the mini coffee maker, begrudgingly lightening his coffee with powdered creamer. He read the news on his tablet, mainly about COVID vaccine mandates and the people rebelling against them. There was also the never-ending news about the deep divisions within the federal government. Gil was conflicted about wanting to get more involved in politics and informing people of how far from good both parties were, but he didn't think he had the energy for it at this point in his life. He switched to Facebook to lower his blood pressure. Mysteriously, there was an ad for kielbasa.

He put on his mask, went down to the lobby, and was thrilled to find a hot breakfast instead of the boxed mini-meals that came about during the pandemic. He opted for healthy choices, getting some eggs, yogurt, and fruit. He brought the meal back up to his room, just to be safe. As he started eating, Micky called.

"After dinner, something was bugging me about your cave, so I talked to my daughter-in-law, Karen. She's a detective for the Greenfield Police Department."

"Well, that's impressive," Gil said.

"Yeah well, in the early nineties, some human remains were discovered in a cave up there, and it could be the same cave. It didn't ring a bell with me back then. Maybe me being back in Greenfield and you talking about your nightmare story made something click. I don't know. Anyway, she said it's still an active case, and she'd like you to give her a call. I'll text you her number."

"Wow, the plot thickens!"

Gil called her, and they agreed to meet at 8:30 a.m. After he finished his breakfast, he headed back up to Poet's Seat Mountain. He parked next to the police car in a small lot at the tower road's entry gate. Karen got out of her car and came over to meet him. She looked to be in her thirties, and she was wearing a police uniform, which surprised Gil. She stayed at a respectful distance and asked if he was Gil.

"Yes, I'm Gil Novak. Hi."

She smiled. "I'm Detective Karen Tindall. Mick told me about your nightmare story last night. Why don't we head to the area where the remains were found, and you can tell me if it's the same place."

She had the location coordinates in her cell phone, and they walked up the access road a few minutes before turning downhill into the woods. They went about a hundred yards downhill before coming to a rise in the terrain, which they circled around. On the other side, an outcropping of red rock jutted out above them. They walked along the rocky base and came to a cleft that opened up into a room-sized cave. "Is this your cave?" she asked.

"It could be. I never actually looked at it from this angle. Let me see if I can find where we were." Gil backtracked along the base of the rock wall and reached a point where he could climb back up above it. He walked along the top of the rise and reached a slight depression in the ground. He knelt down.

"I think this is it. This is where we were! That's our cave!" He dusted himself off and walked back down to the cave entrance. "The day Micky was with me, we saw some people and just took off. The next day when I came back, I was in the same spot and watched for a while. Then someone started shooting at me with a gun. I took off running that way, toward where I parked my bike, but I fell and got knocked out, I think. It was fifty years ago." He let out a laugh, marveling at how insomnia had brought him back here.

"Would you mind coming back to the station with me and making a statement?"

"I'd be happy to. This is so surrealistic!"

FOURTEEN

April 1971—Keeseville, New York

Remi brushed the sawdust from his clothes before going inside. He was proud that he could afford to rent the little white cottage. He was making good money at the sawmill, and he wasn't drinking too much these days. The night terrors from his time in Vietnam didn't come as often. When he walked into the house, little Julian crawled at a fast pace toward him and squealed with delight. Remi scooped him up and bounced him around. Julian drooled all over Remi's old army jacket.

Remi carried him into the kitchen, where Jacqui and Marie sat at the table and suddenly stopped talking. Marie was breastfeeding her newborn, Theo. They were thankful he was born healthy.

Remi noticed Jacqui's dress, and his face went red. "What's this? Where did you go?" Marie looked scared. Jacqui looked defiant.

"I got a job at Pearl's. We need the money."

Remi handed Julian to Marie and slammed both his fists on the table, causing a mug to smash on the floor. Julian started wailing. "I did not agree to this! Your job is here, taking care of the house and your kids. You will not go back there, you hear me?"

Jacqui stood up. "I will go back there. It's a good job and—"

Remi punched her in the face, and she slammed into the wall, blood pouring out of her nose. Marie screamed and ran outside with Julian and Theo. Jacqui recovered after a few seconds and charged toward Remi, but he punched her in the stomach, and she went down, gasping for air.

"You fat pig," Remi yelled. "You're only here to take care of the house and the kids! If you don't do that, you have no reason to live here. Now get my supper!"

_____

Marie was satisfied that things were quieting down, so she carried Julian and Theo over to the picnic table and sat down next to Angela. Angela was whimpering, her shaking hands covering her ears. Marie put her arm around her. "It's okay, Angel. It's over." Angela's body shook and stopped every few seconds, but soon she calmed down. Marie said, "Someday we'll find our way out of this."

_____

Miss Howard could tell that Angela was getting worse. She had pronounced bags under her eyes, and she never smiled anymore. Miss Howard found her alone in the schoolyard and sat next to her. "What's the matter, dear? Why aren't you playing?"

"I don't feel like it."

"You seem sad. What's making you so sad?"

Angela whimpered. "I don't know. I'm just sad."

"Well, I'm just going to have a little talk with your parents."

Angela bolted up from the bench and yelled, "Don't you do that!" Her face was beet red, and her fists were clenched. "You stay away from my parents!"

Miss Howard tried to hug Angela, but Angela twisted away and ran to the other side of the schoolyard.

After school, Miss Howard went to the office and looked in Angela's file for her phone number and address. She told the principal, Mr. Barstow, what was going on and tried to call Angela's parents. The listed phone number was the wrong number. She drove over to Angela's house. When she pulled over, she was confused about which house it was, so she got out and walked up and down the street. The building closest to the address in Angela's file was a small, brick maintenance building of some sort. Miss Howard knocked on the door, but it was clear that nobody was there. A false address.

The next day, Miss Howard decided to follow Angela home from school. She hung back about a hundred yards to make sure she wasn't seen. Angela walked for a ways, her gaze downcast, and then she abruptly cut to the right through some yards. Miss Howard tried to follow, but she decided against climbing over a chain-link fence in her dress. Angela's form faded in the distance. Where was she going?

FIFTEEN

Remi powered down the buzz saw, then trudged through the April mud to the Dog House—the shed where everyone took their lunch breaks when the weather was unpleasant. Bracing against the chill, he scraped the mud from the soles of his boots and hurried inside. The other guys were already eating, and all the seats were taken. There should have been at least two more. Remi's surprise didn't go unnoticed, which is why Kelso couldn't help but snicker. He was sitting next to Metz, Remi's tormentor.

"I guess the Canuck's gonna have to eat outside," Metz said. Some of the others chuckled.

Remi dropped his lunchbox and launched himself at Metz. He got a couple of good shots at Metz's face before Metz kneed him in the groin. Remi stopped to let the pain wash over him, and Metz laughed. Remi barreled back into Metz and pushed his head into the side of the hot wood stove. Metz screamed, and the others ran out of the shed.

The foreman, Carl Taylor, ran over to quell the commotion. A huge guy, Carl had no trouble throwing the two men out of the shed. "Get your stuff and go home. You assholes are fired!"

"He started it!" Remi said. "He was fucking with me! I've got kids."

"You know the rules Remi, and this wasn't the first time. You assholes are fired! Now get out of here."

———

Remi spent the afternoon at Dice's Bar. Except for a few retirees, hardly anybody was there until the sun started to go down, and by then Remi had drunk enough to discover he was hungry. He stumbled to his car and drove the several blocks home. He hit his elbow trying to get through the front door, sending searing pain through his arm. Jacqui was in the kitchen with the girls, and they were surprised to see him in such a state. He'd all but sobered up the last couple of years.

"A sorry excuse for a man," Jacqui said. Angela grabbed Julian and ran to her room.

Remi grabbed Jacqui and punched her in the stomach. Her face turned red, and she couldn't breathe. Remi opened the back door, kicked her down the back steps, and slammed the door shut. Marie went to the back door, but Remi strode to her with his fist raised. "Don't you open that fucking door! You make me some food—now!" He went to his chair in the living room and passed out.

Marie quietly walked down the hall into Angela's room. Julian was squealing with delight as he peeled a corner of the wallpaper off the wall. Theo was napping in Marie's room. Angela was shaking and whimpering. Marie put her arms around her sister and said, "It's all over, Angel. It's all over."

———————

Remi woke to Marie screaming at him. "She's dead! She's dead! You killed her, you bastard!"

He jumped out of his chair, and pain pierced his head. He grabbed the wall to steady himself and went out the back door. Jacqui lay right where she landed. He felt for a pulse on her neck, but there was none. She was very cold and felt as though she were made of rubber. He ran back into the house and grabbed Marie's arm. "You and Angela, get all of your stuff into the car. We're leaving." She looked at him like he was crazy. "NOW!"

SIXTEEN

June 2021—Greenfield, Massachusetts

After writing and signing his witness statement, Gil took a ride to the pumping station, an old hangout from his youth. A covered bridge traversed the Green River there, but the whole area was fenced off, which made him feel disappointed. He remembered that somebody had burned down the original bridge when he was young and that it had been rebuilt.

Nearby, a historical marker about Eunice Williams described her capture by Native Americans during their infamous raid on the nearby town of Deerfield during Queen Anne's War. She was killed near the pumping station as she and other captives were marched toward Canada. All the students in Greenfield had to learn about the area's history, and they took field trips to Old Deerfield to make the history come alive. Gil was taught this history through the eyes of the settlers, but not at all through the eyes of the Native Americans. He hoped that had changed.

After crossing the bridge, Gil headed south along the Green River toward the Greenfield Swimming Pool, the dammed-up area of the river where he had taught himself to swim. He pulled over to check it out and was pleased to see that it had been updated and well-maintained. It wasn't very crowded, and he laughed to himself as he thought about Eddie Locke's mud dance fantasy up around the river bend.

He took a ride east out of town and stopped just below the large dam on the Connecticut River. He found a path that led him down a rocky slope to the shore. Just a trickle of water was coming through the dam, probably just enough to keep the ecosystem alive. As kids, Gil and his friends would listen to cassette tapes of rock music and catch fish there. The water in that area looked clean back then because it was upstream of the nearby factories, but he was suspicious of how clean it really was.

He climbed back up the slope and rode through downtown Turner's Falls, the village on the other side of the river from Greenfield. It looked less depressed than when he was young, and it seemed to have some good little restaurants. There still wasn't much to the downtown area, though. He pulled a U-turn and rode into the park along Barton's Cove, which was the small lake formed above the dam. The park and the cove looked pleasant, and a few motorboats were cutting through the water. He walked back to the main drag and decided to get a vanilla ice cream cone for lunch. He preferred chocolate but avoided it due to his insomnia. Then his phone rang. He fumbled around, trying to answer it while keeping his ice cream from dripping. Detective Tindall invited him back to the police station to meet the chief.

Chief Manny Reyes looked like he wanted to shake Gil's hand, but he just gave him a head nod and indicated for him to sit in the chair across from his desk. Detective Tindall sat next to Gil. They all wore face masks.

"Detective Tindall filled me in on your tale of adventure and how it ties to one of our cold cases," said Chief Reyes. "We used a metal detector to confirm your story. There were bullets right where you said they would be. And there was another detail: you mentioned a deformed child. The remains we found were those of a deformed child, a fact that we never released to the public."

Gil said, "Holy moly, how about that!"

Reyes chuckled. "Detective Tindall suggested that we ask you to consult on this case. We don't have much manpower to assign to it, and you have expertise in this area."

"Expertise?" Gil asked.

"Well, for one thing, you were actually there at the scene of the crime. We don't consider you a suspect. You were just a kid with no motive who got shot at. But we also don't have anybody who has a feel for what things were like back then. You know, hippies and such. Also, it's an old cold case that nobody but us is interested in. We did a background check on you. You have high-level security clearance. Your boss practically worships you. He says you're a genius at making robots."

"Chet's being overly dramatic. I've designed manufacturing robots for my whole career. Over the years, I worked on some projects for the Department of Defense, but I'm sure my clearance will expire soon."

Karen leaned in. "We need to track down some former hippie people and try to identify this family and their acquaintances."

"This isn't Los Angeles," said Reyes, "so we don't have a budget for fancy consultants. But we can pay some of your expenses from the funds we have for victims of violent crimes and crime witnesses."

"I wasn't really the victim here," Gil said.

"You've suffered from PTSD ever since you were a child," Karen said. "You're definitely a victim—at the very least, a witness. And as far as this crime goes, there's somebody out there who may have killed a young child and someone who was willing to kill you with a gun. Maybe there was one killer or maybe more than one, but there may be some dangerous people out there, even after all these years. What do you say?"

Gil thought about it for a few seconds. "Sure, I'll do it. I'll have to go back home and get some more clothes. When do you want to start?"

"How about Monday?"

"Okay, I'll be here sometime Monday morning."

SEVENTEEN

April 1971—Crown Point, New York

Remi nervously paid the toll and crossed over the Lake Champlain Bridge into Vermont, breathing a sigh of relief. He didn't know how long it would take for the police to discover Jacqui's body, but it would take a while for the Vermont staties to find out about it. Even longer for Massachusetts Police.

The kids slept soundly as he drove through the night, only waking when he stopped for gas. He bought a New England road map, some cigarettes, chips and twinkies, then continued on his way. He took the back roads around Middlebury and headed south and east. Eventually he reached a gravel area where he could pull off to the side of the road and stay out of sight for a brief sleep.

A piercing scream woke Remi. Julian needed tending. The girls stirred, and he told them to change the babies' diapers and feed them. The sun had risen, but it was cold. Remi tried to start the car to get the heat going, but it took several tries for the engine to catch. They hit the road again, munching on junk food.

————————

The air quickly warmed up from the bright spring sun as Remi continued driving southeast. Surrounded by forests and a few small farms, the road meandered alongside hills and a stream. When he encountered an area with many cars parked along both sides of the road, he pulled over. They all got out and followed a group of hippies through the trees to a cascading waterfall. Below the falls, the stream was filled with skinny-dipping hippies. Along the banks were small groups of nude sunbathers. Marie and Angela burst out laughing.

Remi approached a guy who still had his clothes on. "Excuse me, what is this place?"

"Hey, man! This is the gorge! Come and party with us, man." The girls stayed up on the hill, watching the spectacle while Remi followed the guy down to his group of friends. They were mostly naked and passed around a massive joint. Remi had seen guys smoking marijuana in the Army, but he never tried it. He chatted and smoked for a while to find out more about these people. "Why did you guys become hippies?" he finally asked.

A girl with big frizzy hair said, "We were sick of living with the old rules, so now we're happy. Instead of being tied down like our parents, we go where we want, party when we want, and make love whenever and with whoever we want." Remi couldn't imagine having sex with such a hairy girl.

A naked guy with dark hair all over his body said, "Man, after two years in 'Nam, I knew I didn't fit in back home. I was just looking for something different, you know?"

A girl with long, red hair asked, "What's your gig?"

"My wife just died, so me and my daughters are looking for a change. Something different, I guess."

"That's tough, man," said the red-haired girl. "Are you headed to the commune?"

"Commune? What's that?"

The frizzy-haired girl said, "Communes are autonomous collectives where people work together for the good of the

61

community. Sometimes I live at the Astral Plane Commune, and it's cool. You should check it out."

"Where is that commune? Is it near here?"

"Not too far. It's near Farnum, I think. A ways past Greenfield."

While they were smoking and chatting, Remi noticed a young teenage girl wading in the stream, and he couldn't take his eyes off her. After staring at the girl for maybe too long, he realized that he was feeling really stoned, and he liked it. He bought a bag of pot for ten dollars, and they threw in a packet of rolling papers for him. Remi went up the hill to the girls and said, "I'm really stoned, Marie. You drive." He handed her the car keys.

"I can't drive," said Marie. "I don't have a license, and I don't know how!"

"Well, it's about time you learned. Let's go."

Marie pushed down the gas pedal and turned the key. The starter motor turned over, but the engine didn't catch. She stopped, and there was a strong smell of gasoline.

"Aw, you flooded it." Remi only seemed a little concerned. "We need to wait five minutes and try it again. Only step on the gas a little when you start it."

Marie waited a few minutes and tried again. This time the engine started up, but she was still gunning it.

"Whoa, take your foot off the gas once it's started. That's it. Let it warm up for a minute so it doesn't stall out. Now put your foot on the brake and shift it into Drive."

They got going down the road, moving very slowly. Whenever a car came from the other way, Marie swerved to the shoulder. Remi remained fast asleep. After a while, she became more confident and was going closer to the speed limit. She passed a sign welcoming them to Massachusetts, and the terrain seemed to flatten out to open farmland with cows, sheep, and horses. A few miles later, she reached the town of Colrain, which seemed like nothing more than a few houses. She crossed a small bridge over a stream and came to a fork in the road. She stopped, and the car behind her beeped its horn, but she didn't know what to do. She nudged Remi awake and said, "Which way do I go?" The driver kept beeping at her, eventually passing by and yelling at her.

"Pull over to the side," said Remi. He looked at his map, saw which way most of the cars were going, and said, "Go to the left. Go to Greenfield." And he went back to sleep.

Marie continued driving on a rural road surrounded by forests, farms, and orchards. She thought about pulling over and taking off while her dad slept, but they were in the middle of nowhere. Sometime soon they would get the chance. She pulled over to a farm stand that was selling eggs and flowers. Marie showed her map to a teenage girl with scraggly blonde hair and said, "Hi, um, could you tell me where I am on here?"

The girl looked over the map and said, "You're right here. You want me to mark it?" She grabbed a pencil and put a dot where they were and circled it. "Where are you headed?"

"I guess we're headed to this town here, Greenfield. Would we just keep going until we hit Route 2?"

"You could, but there's a shortcut. In about a mile and a half, take a left on Brook Road and just keep going. I don't think that road has a sign, so you might miss it, but that's not a big deal. After a while, you'll hit Route 2 anyway, so you just take a left there, and you'll end up on Main Street."

"Okay, thanks!" Marie did as she was told, but after a while, Brook Road became a scary dirt road. It was full of potholes, rocks, and curves as it followed the brook, with sections narrowed due to wash-outs. They were deep in a dark forest surrounded by steep hills and trees that had been toppled by landslides. She went slowly, but the shock absorbers were creaking severely.

The violent movements of the car combined with the shrieking cries of both babies finally woke Remi. He grabbed onto the car in fear. "What's happening?" Angela stirred.

Marie kept her eyes focused on the road. "We're on a shortcut to Greenfield, but it's really rough."

He saw that nobody was following them so he said, "Stop the car!" He took over the driving, and very soon the road became smooth, paved, and surrounded by well-kept farms. Then the car shook violently for a few seconds and died. Remi slammed his hands on the steering wheel. "God damn it!" Marie helped Remi push it to the side of the road, where he opened the hood. A small amount of smoke came off the engine. He unscrewed the oil cap, and he fell on his butt when it shot high into the air. More smoke poured out. "Get everybody out of the car!" he yelled.

The oil cap was smoldering in the field, so Remi grabbed a rag from under his car seat and picked it up. This was bad news. He put the cap back where it belonged and said, "We have to walk. We can only take what we can carry."

"We can't carry all this stuff," said Marie. "We have to carry the babies!"

Remi looked at the map and asked Marie to show him where they were. "Here," she said, pointing. They'd need to head east after Greenfield. "Let's just take what we need for now, and we'll walk to town and ask for help. We gotta be close." Remi was worried. He was glad that he had some money. He didn't trust banks, so he always kept all of his money in his wallet. They grabbed what they needed, locked the car, and started walking into town.

EIGHTEEN

June 2021—Greenfield, Massachusetts

Karen brought Gil into a meeting room to display her computer on the large monitor. She told Gil that the child died of a broken neck, but they couldn't tell whether it was a murder or an accident. Their first goal was to identify the child and his family, and he helped her create a digital murder board similar to the physical ones he'd seen on TV. The board included everything Gil thought he remembered about the family from his hypnosis sessions.

"I'm working with Agent Lili D'Amico at the State Police Crime Lab in Springfield," said Karen. "I've sent the bullets down for ballistic analysis. We still have the child's remains for some reason, even though they should have been buried a long time ago, so I sent those down too. I've tried searching the internet for hippies living in caves, but I didn't find anything about that in this area. What I'd like you to do next is figure out who we could talk to from the hippie community to try and identify this family."

"I can do that. A lot of it will involve the communes in this area. The hippies gravitated toward them. One thing I'm curious about, though. How were the remains discovered, and what did the police find, back in the nineties?"

"There was a group of middle schoolers on a geology field trip. They were rooting around, looking for different minerals, and one of the kids uncovered the bones. It must have been shocking for the kids. The police investigation found no useful leads. By the way, you're invited to Mick's house for a cookout tonight at six thirty. You game?"

"That sounds great!"

Nobody was wearing masks at the cookout. Micky's wife was named Jane, and she was a lawyer specializing in women's advocacy. She introduced Gil to her sons and daughters. Her son Jeff was Karen's husband. After Gil got a plate of food, he sat down at the picnic table. Jane sat down with him and started pumping him for information about his life while he was fumbling around, trying to eat ribs and corn on the cob. "I'm so sorry to hear about Cynthia," she said.

"Thanks. It's been about a year, and I'm just starting to come out of my funk." She asked him question after question about his kids and grandkids, his engineering work, and his late wife. At a certain point, Gil felt like she knew more about him than he did—including how much barbecue sauce was on his face. He was about to ask Jane about herself, but she abruptly got up and said she had to go check on something. The food was great, and he was considering seconds when a back slap nearly knocked the wind out of him. "Oh. Hi, Eddie." Gil stood up to talk to him.

"So Gil, I hear you've suddenly become a gumshoe, a sleuth, a private eye, a *dick*!"

"No, I'm just helping out a little. I'm just a high-priced consultant."

Eddie wagged his finger. "A lot of people around here are going to be pretty twitchy about that. You know where the proverbial bodies are buried around here, after all." He poked Gil in the chest. "You just remember, buddy, we have stuff on you too. I know who egged Damon Barne's Triumph. I know who put the dead skunk in the girl's room at the high school. I know who blew up an M-80 in Needle-Nose Garber's mailbox. You better think twice about what you say and to whom you say it!"

Gil laughed. "Eddie, *you* blew up Mr. Garber's mailbox." Mr. Garber was the much-feared vice principal of their junior high school. He had a sharp protruding nose and would get up in your face when he was mad at you.

"Oh yeah, I guess I did. So I do know who did it then, don't I?" Eddie wiggled his eyebrows, then suddenly became more composed. "So you and Mick saw who killed the cave boy . . ."

"No, we just saw some people around up there, so maybe the police can figure out who he is and what happened to him. Do you know any old hippies from back then?"

"Nah, but those were the days, weren't they? Free love, acid trips, rock 'n' roll, lava lamps—yeah baby! Of course, at our age now, there's no greater pleasure than taking a good dump."

Gil laughed. "You could write a song about that."

"Oh, here comes my lovely friend Pam. Pam, this is Gil, who we saw at the country club."

Gil smiled. "Nice to meet you, Pam. Are you going to the mud dance?"

She looked at me quizzically, and Eddie said, "Um, uh, Gil must be a little confused. I can explain."

Jane came back and interrupted. "Eddie, do you mind if I borrow Gil for a few minutes? Official business." Gil got up, and Jane led him to a corner of the yard where they couldn't be heard. "Karen asked if I could find the names of anybody connected to the hippy community. I gave her a couple of names, but one woman told me she might know something, but she wasn't willing to talk to the police. I explained who you were and asked if she'd be willing to talk to you, and she said she would." She pressed a note into his hand with a name and number.

"Thanks, Jane."

NINETEEN

The next morning, Karen and Gil were adding information to their murder board. Karen told Gil about the two contacts that Jane gave her. "I checked out their histories," she said, "and both got busted for marijuana possession back in the sixties and seventies. Both did a little jail time for, like, a few days. Carter Billings lives in Hadley, and Tina Renaldi lives in Shelburne. I suggest we go talk to them. So far, the others you found online yesterday turned out to be deceased."

Gil handed her Jane's note. "Here, check this one out. Jane said that this girl, Lexi Florakis, doesn't want to talk to the police. But she agreed to talk with me. Perhaps I should talk to her alone."

Jane looked cross. "First of all, this 'girl' is probably in her seventies, so maybe calling her a woman would be more appropriate."

Gil chuckled. "I'm sorry, you're right. Sometimes I have trouble updating my terminology. Please slap me upside the head if I screw up again."

Karen rolled her eyes. "Here she is. She doesn't have a record, and she lives in New Castle, New Hampshire. Let's see how these other folks are, and we'll decide if it's safe for you to go to New Castle on your own."

It took a half hour for Karen to drive to Hadley. Gil only knew this town for its malls and big-box stores, but Carter

Billings lived in a beautiful big farmhouse on a scenic road along the Connecticut River. Carter introduced Karen and Gil to his wife Terry; both looked to be in their mid-seventies. Sitting inside their screened-in porch, Gil squinted at the yellow-flowered plants in rows behind the house and asked, "Pumpkins?"

"Yep, pumpkins and butternut squash. I don't farm, but I lease the land to a farmer. So, Detective, you said you want to talk about the commune?"

"We're trying to track down the family of a child whose remains were found in Greenfield back in the nineties. It's a cold case. Mr. Novak here is a consultant to the Greenfield Police Department. You were in the Farnum commune?"

"A cold case with a consultant. This sounds like a TV show. Both Terry and I were in the Astral Plane Commune in Farnum." Terry brought them a tray of lemonade and started pouring.

"The family may have included a very young woman, possibly a teenager, who had a baby, and there was another girl, about twelve years old. Both girls had straight dark hair."

Carter thought a moment and rubbed his chin. "Well, it's been fifty years . . ."

"I remember 'em," said Terry. "Those girls were afraid of their father. The young mother was named after a plant or a tree—Willow or something like that, I think. She had a hippie name." Terry sat down.

"You said the man was the father of the young mother?" Karen asked.

"Yes," said Terry. "And the father of that baby too, I think. I helped them escape."

71

"I remember that!" said Carter. "We drove them to the Leverett Farm one night. There was a kid that died? Did you know that?"

"No! I only thought they were scared because their father was abusing them. He was intent on raping the younger girl since she was starting to, uh, develop. Oh my God, those poor kids!"

Karen finished writing her notes. "Can you describe the father, or anything else about the girls and their babies?"

Terry said, "There were just two girls and one baby. I remember that the father was a lot older than us, maybe in his thirties. Almost everybody in the commune was in their late teens or early twenties back then. He had short-ish dark hair and a small beard."

"Those were the early days," said Carter. "Maybe seventy or seventy-one. People were coming and going all the time. I was in charge of construction, so I would put some of the men to work clearing land, laying pipes, and running wires. We were building dormitories and workshops. Other guys did maintenance, cleaning, and farming. There were a lot of guys that weren't there long enough for me to remember them. We had rules against drugs and alcohol, but some guys were troublemakers. Thankfully, there was another guy, Seth Wheeler, in charge of security."

"Do you know how I can contact Mr. Wheeler?" Karen asked.

Carter shook his head. "Nah, we didn't stay in touch."

"We get posts about the commune once in a while on a Facebook page. Maybe you could track Seth down that way. The younger girl would have needed to go to school. The commune started its own school, but I think that would have been later on. The girl with the baby may have been put to work in childcare. I was in charge of printing T-shirts for the band, so I don't remember them very well."

"T-shirts for a band?" asked Karen.

Not wanting to waste time, Gil chimed in and said, "The commune was connected to a rock band. I'll show you the background material when we get back to the station. When did you leave the commune, and what did you do? You have a very nice house."

Carter smiled at the compliment. "After being in charge of construction at the commune, which turned out to be a very big deal, I left in 1975 and started my own construction company here. I built a lot of the commercial properties you see on Route 9."

"I left with Carter," Terry said. "I was a social studies teacher at the high school in Amherst."

Karen asked, "Terry, how did you find out that the girls were in trouble and needed to escape?"

Terry thought for a while and said, "I don't remember exactly. Some of the women were kind of shuffling them along and were looking for someone to get those kids out of there. They said the father was trying to rape the younger daughter. The family stood out because we hardly had any kids around back then. I was hanging out with Carter, and we just sort of jumped into action." She thought about it for a few seconds and said, "I can't really remember who was there at the time."

"You mentioned bringing them to the Leverett Farm. Where was that?"

"That was another, much smaller commune," said Carter. "Not many people knew about them." He showed them a map of the Leverett Farm on his laptop.

"Is there anything else you remember that could help us?" Karen asked. Nobody said anything.

Gil asked, "Whatever happened to the leader of the commune?

Carter chuckled. "His name was Vincent Held. He was kind of forced out of the commune by the people who were running it. He was wasting money and diverging from the ideals people wanted to pursue. Anyway, he ended up being an appliance repairman in the area. He died a long time ago. Gil had a surprised look on his face.

Karen stood up. "Well, we won't take any more of your time. Thank you so much for speaking with us. This has been very helpful." She handed Carter her card. "Please call me if you think of anything else I should know. I have a lot of studying to do about these communes. Terry, could you get me the link to that commune Facebook page?"

TWENTY

When Karen knocked on Tina Renaldi's door, a yappy dog inside went apoplectic. The house was small and white, with a one-car garage, a neatly trimmed yard, and an impressive garden. Karen introduced Gil and herself, showed her identification, and Tina welcomed them in. Tina was a very petite woman in her seventies and wore a tank top and very short hot-pink shorts. The inside of her house was shocking to Gil—it seemed like the inside of a tropical bamboo hut. It had dark wicker walls and ceilings, loads of palm-like and banana-leafed plants, rainbow-colored birds in and out of cages, and hanging beads. New Age music played, and floral scents filled the air. "Wow!" Gil said.

"Yeah, it's a little overwhelming for most people," said Tina. "But it's what I like. Please have a seat. Can I get you anything?"

"No thanks," said Karen. "We're good. As I said on the phone, we're interested in tracking down someone from the commune days. We're investigating a cold case involving the remains of a child found at Poet's Seat Mountain back in the nineties. We're trying to find his family and figure out what happened to him."

"Can't you just trace the child's DNA?"

"We're working on that, but that takes a long time, not like on TV. Also, it often doesn't tell us anything unless a close relative is in a database we can access. In the meantime, we're chasing other leads. We think this family came through some of the communes around 1970 or 1971. There was a young teenage girl, possibly named Willow, who had a baby, and another girl around twelve years old." Karen checked her notes. "Maybe they came through the Peace Out Commune in Vermont. We understand you were there back then."

"We called it Fipp's Corners. That's the local name for the area. Those were the early days, and we didn't have many people yet. Maybe thirty? There were always a lot of transient hippies coming through who I wouldn't remember. There weren't any kids back then. The kids came later." She smiled to herself.

"These girls were scared of their father," said Gil. "He may have been abusing them."

Tina shook her head. "I don't remember them. I'm sorry. I was hard at work back then. I did a lot of farm work and was trying out different forms of art. I wish I still had that much energy. You know, a few years later, our commune started a shelter for abused women in Brattleboro. Those young girls you're talking about weren't the only ones. We created sort of an underground railroad for women back then, but that was maybe in seventy-three or seventy-four."

"What was the name of the women's shelter?" Karen asked. "Maybe they have records?"

"It was called the Brookside Shelter. Back in the early days, we didn't have much in the way of record-keeping, but we did keep a log. Every now and then, the cops used to come by, looking for someone who was missing. We sort of started writing down information that would help. But a lot of times it was the abusive husband looking for his wife so he could hurt her."

Gil asked, "What did you do after you left the commune?"

"I went back to UMass and got my degree. I spent my career as a social worker for the state, but I retired eleven years ago."

———————————

Karen and Gil stopped at a Middle Eastern restaurant for lunch. "So, consultant, what do you think about these interviews?"

"I'm surprised anybody remembered this family at all. Those girls must have been really scared to make an impression on Terry and Carter. I think everybody's been telling the truth, but I don't have a lot of experience reading people. I mostly worked with machines. That said, a lot of the commune hippies were idealists back then. Sure, there were some bad apples, but in general they were very peaceful people."

"Well, I guess I'm okay with you visiting Ms. Florakis on your own. There doesn't seem to be any animosity associated with this case."

"Yeah, I'm okay with it too."

TWENTY-ONE

Early the next morning, Gil was on his motorcycle headed east on Route 2, wary of predicted thunderstorms. The rising sun was occasionally right in his eyes, which annoyed him. He reminded himself that the sun wasn't actually rising; the earth was spinning toward the east.

The scenery was beautiful as he rode along the Millers River, which looked like the ideal fly-fishing stream. It looked clean now, despite being terribly polluted when Gil was young.

———————————

Gil looked up and saw two big brown eyes floating in the fog. A bright light hit his eyes. He heard beeping and mumbled voices. The fog quickly cleared, and he realized he was in a hospital bed. A woman with big brown eyes and brown skin said, "Don't try to speak. You have a tube down your throat. You've been in an accident, but you're going to be fine. We'll remove your breathing tube in a few minutes."

Gil fell back to sleep.

He woke up again, and a few minutes later, a young man came into the room and looked him over. The young man called a doctor, who turned out to be the woman with the big brown eyes. Everyone wore blue surgical masks.

"Hi, Mr. Novak. I'm Doctor McNaughton. I'm going to remove your breathing tube now. While I pull it out, I'd like you to cough." She pulled, he coughed, he took a deep breath, it hurt.

"Hurt," Gil croaked. Gil gestured for something to drink, so the nurse brought him a cup of water with a straw, which he sipped.

"I'll adjust your pain meds in a minute. You are at Baystate Medical Center in Springfield. You were in a motorcycle accident. You have a chest injury, a broken left collarbone, two broken fingers on your left hand, and scrapes and bruises on your left hip and leg. Your helmet saved your life. You're going to be fine, eventually. Do you have any questions for me?"

It took some effort, but after a few seconds Gil whispered, "Dr. McNaughton, you don't look Irish."

The doctor and the young man looked at each other and cracked up. "Now I'm sure you're going to be okay." She asked him some questions to assess his pain and told the nurse to give him some medicine.

After they left, Karen came in looking distraught. "This is all my fault, Gil. I'm so sorry. I shouldn't have let you go alone. You could have been killed."

He was drowsy. "What happened? Why your fault?" He fell asleep as she started to answer.

Gil woke up a few times during the night as nurses came and went. When he woke up in the morning, his daughter Julia was there. "How are you feeling?" She looked shaken.

"I feel doped up. How are you? What are you doing here?"

"What are you doing playing detective? You could have been killed!"

"I don't remember what happened. I could have been in an accident anywhere. I'm just helping the cops a little with a cold case."

"The detective said it wasn't an accident. She said someone stretched a rope across the road."

Gil was shocked at first, but then he said. "If you're catching flak, you know you're over the target."

"What's that mean?"

Gil sucked some water from his straw and said, "During World War II, the Allies did constant bombing raids over Germany, but navigation equipment was rudimentary back then. It was often cloudy, and they couldn't tell if they were over their targets. But they knew they were in the right place when they started catching antiaircraft fire—flak."

"Huh. What's all this about, anyway?"

"In the early nineties, the bones of a child were discovered in a cave up on Poet's Seat Mountain. It turns out that when I was a teenager back in the early seventies, I saw that child with his family at that cave. I was able to provide a lead in this cold case. The police asked me to assist them because I speak hippy."

"That sounds like the plot of a horror movie. Well, I think your detecting days are over."

"How's my bike?"

"I don't know, you can't ride it anyway!" Julia snapped. "The doctor says I might be able to take you home tomorrow if you're stable for another day."

"In the front left pocket of my jeans, wherever they are, is my hotel room key at the Hampton Inn. Go explain what happened to the hotel people, and you can stay there tonight. Thanks for coming. I think I need to take a nap."

TWENTY-TWO

April 1971—Keeseville, New York

Mike Gorman strolled along the sidewalk, smoking his tobacco pipe while his aging German shepherd, Sheila, followed along. He'd lived in Keeseville all his life, except for the couple of years he spent fighting the Nazis in Europe. They gave him his limp. The bright spring sunshine was pleasant in the cool air. He looked back and caught a glimpse of Sheila's tail disappearing around the corner of the house he just walked by. "Sheila, come here!" he called out. She didn't reappear, so he followed her and saw her nudging a person who had fallen.

He quickly went over and put his hand on the woman's shoulder, giving her a little shake. "Are you all right, miss?" She was cold to the touch and didn't respond. He felt for a pulse but didn't find one. There was a small puddle of congealed blood below her face. "Oh my God," he said to himself. He took off his jacket and covered her, then he went to the back door, knocking and yelling. Nobody responded. He ran out front and saw a woman across the street letting her cat out, so he called out to her, but she had already shut the door.

He ran up and desperately knocked on her door. She answered and he said, "There's a young woman out behind that house, and I think she might be dead! We need to call the police!"

"Oh my God! Come in, Come in!" she said. She ran over to a yellow rotary phone on the kitchen wall and she said, "The number is on the sticker."

Mike told the police what he'd seen, and they asked for the address. "What's the number of that house?" he asked the neighbor.

She looked out the front door, then said, "Forty-two."

Mike relayed it and hung up, and the woman followed him back across the street. "What's your name?"

"Don't you remember me, Mike? I'm Ginny Cross, Helen Markham's sister. Oh my! That's Jacqui. Jacqui Foy."

"Oh, I do remember you! I went to school with Helen." They heard a siren, then saw a sheriff patrol car coming down the street. Mike waved them down, and two deputies followed him to the back of the house. One asked Ginny to wait out front for the ambulance, so Ginny went.

Deputy LeBrun introduced himself while steering Mike a distance away and asked him what happened. Mike told them what he knew. "Is she dead?" he asked at the end.

"She might be, but that's not for me to say. I asked dispatch if the ambulance could bring a doctor or a nurse." In that area, ambulance drivers were not yet trained to give medical assistance, only transport.

The ambulance pulled up, and a nurse ran out back with an equipment bag. She threw aside Mike's jacket and listened with her stethoscope. "She's alive, but just barely. I'm gonna start an IV. She checked her head and neck. Help me turn her over." Deputy LeBrun helped her. The nurse got the IV going, and the ambulance crew loaded her into the ambulance on a gurney.

The other deputy came out of the back door. "Nobody's home."

Deputy LeBrun sighed. "Mike, do you know this woman?"

"No, but Ginny does." Mike grabbed his jacket off the ground and petted Sheila for being a good dog. The deputies questioned Ginny for a few minutes. As they all were leaving, Ginny asked, "Hey, Mike, would you like a cup of coffee? I'm still shaking."

TWENTY-THREE

June 2021—Saratoga Springs, New York

Two weeks after leaving the hospital, Gil was in Julia's backyard for grilled salmon. His arm was in a sling, and his hand was splinted and bandaged. His chest didn't hurt as much. He still walked with a limp, and he was trying to avoid his granddaughters, who seemed determined to knock him over. Julia came out of the house with Karen Tindall in tow. She was wearing civilian clothes.

"Karen! What the heck are you doing here, way out of your jurisdiction?"

She had a serious look on her face. "I need to talk to you in private. Can we just go out front for a few minutes?" His cheerfulness gave way to concern. He followed her toward the front of the house.

Karen walked slowly so he could keep up. When they got to the driveway, a tall, handsome man was standing there smiling, and there was Gil's bike, good as new. "My bike!"

"You remember my husband Jeff?"

"Hi, Gil!" said Jeff. "Your bike rides like a dream! I've always been a Harley guy, but now I'm not so sure."

"Thanks for riding it all the way out here for me. I can't believe it's fixed up already! I'm still broken."

Karen said, "Chief Reyes had the department spring for the repairs, so it shouldn't cause your insurance to go up."

Jeff said, "Donny, the bike repair guy, said the frame is fine, so it's probably in better shape than when you bought it."

"Well, it might be a while till I can ride it. Come on back and have some food!"

———————————

Gil introduced Karen and Jeff to everyone and made sure that they got some food. Jeff got to chatting with Mike. Mike was a financial advisor, so everyone liked talking to him. Julia was the office manager at the local airport's fixed-base operator. Both Karen and Julia had fascinating jobs, but they were talking about their kids when Gil joined them.

After a couple of minutes, Karen said, "Gil, when we started the investigation, we jumped right into it, but I never had a chance to ask you what the hippies were like back in the day. I researched the communes and learned a little about life back then, but not so much about the people."

Gil said, "Well, I was just a teenager, but I had a pretty good sense of things. My house was on Federal Street, so a lot of times I would see groups of hippies walking by. In fact, things were pretty boring back then, so sometimes my friends would come over, and we'd all sit on my front porch for the afternoon just to watch the hippies go by."

Karen and Julia looked at him like he was crazy.

He smiled sheepishly. "They just abandoned their old lives—school, work, or whatever—and they roamed the country to seek out like-minded people. Some were into free love and drugs, and some were politically active, protesting the Vietnam War, pollution, racial inequality—things like that. Some were into music and formed bands or folk groups. Some were into spiritualism and experimented with Buddhism,

Hinduism, and New Age stuff. Some were into the commune life, farming, making cheese or food, and some were into arts and crafts, making and selling jewelry or candles—that sort of thing. I think they just wanted to make the world a better place, and I think they actually did.

"Since there were a lot of communes in the area, some of the people who lived in town formed loose connections with them. Some of my teachers got in trouble for using or selling drugs. One even got fired for getting pregnant while being single." Julia and Karen looked at each other, mouths agape. "I knew one guy who had a local band. We would watch them practice, and then they'd go into the woods to drop acid and make out with their girlfriends."

"Did you take drugs back then?" Julia asked.

"No, I didn't even drink alcohol, but some of the kids in high school did drink. A few smoked pot. I did try pot in college, though. I didn't like it. It makes people lethargic. I did get to see the Starshine band play once at the bandshell opposite the skating rink. That was the band from the Astral Plane Commune."

"Bandshell?" asked Karen.

"Yeah, there was a big green wooden bandshell where the old veterans' band played weekly concerts in the summer. Anyway, the Starshine band was very good. They sang a lot of harmonies like Crosby, Stills, and Nash." Karen and Julia looked like they had no clue.

As Karen and Jeff were leaving, Karen said, "I didn't want to say this in front of your family, but Manny and I are hoping you'll come back and visit when you feel up to it. There's a lot more interest in the investigation since someone tried to kill you. I'd like you to look at what we have, and maybe you'll have some ideas."

TWENTY-FOUR

June 2021—Greenfield, Massachusetts

It was 3:17 a.m. when Karen's phone rang. "Tindall," she croaked.

"Karen, this is Manny. We got an arson at the middle school, in the back. It was a small fire and it's out. Let me know what you find."

She was out the door in twenty minutes and at the scene in five minutes more. Sergeant Phillips and Officer Jupe were there, along with the fire department. Phillips said, "It looks like someone broke a ground-level window, poured some gas in the building, and lit it. But they spilled gas on the ground outside, and the gas can caught fire and blew up. There was nothing around to catch fire."

"Whoever did it could have gotten burned," said Jupe. "Maybe it was kids."

Fire Chief Don LaFarge and Principal Emily Whitset walked over. LaFarge said, "Hi, Karen. Luckily there wasn't anybody in the building, and there wasn't much damage. Come on over and take a look." There was a thirty-foot oval of burned grass behind the paved walkway that abutted the building. Next to the broken window was a melted lump of red-and-black plastic that would have been the gas can. "It looks like they lit some sticks with a lighter, then threw the sticks through the broken window. The gas that spilled around the can would have caught fire right away. Hopefully, they backed off before the gas can blew up."

Karen said to Phillips, "You guys check with the hospital and see if they got a burn victim. I'll get some pictures and collect the evidence. Who called it in?"

Jupe said, "I did. I saw it while I was driving by. I didn't see any other witnesses around. In the morning, we'll ask the neighbors if they saw anything. There are only a few houses that could have seen anything."

Karen turned to Principal Whitset. "When you can, please get me a list of students who are absent today or anybody that looks like they got burned."

"I'll get you that in the morning, but right now we could look at our surveillance cameras."

In the office, they started looking at the six external camera feeds simultaneously, starting a half hour before the reported fire. "It looks like there's a blind spot between cameras four and five," said Principal Whitset. The cameras only monitored the grounds and the front entryway. The broken window and the whole walkway adjacent to the building were in the blind spot.

Karen noticed a flash of red and stopped the video. "That looks like a corner of the gas can. Where are we looking?"

"That's on an angle at the back toward Sanderson Street. If you click here, you can get a still picture of that frame."

Karen resumed the video. They spotted several more glimpses, an elbow, a piece of a shoe, and the top of a head. Karen captured still photos of each of them. "Well, we know two things. One of the arsonists has short hair, and they know where the camera blind spots are. Can you get me a copy of these files?"

———————

Karen sauntered into the station at a little after ten o'clock, surprised that she was able to get a few more hours of sleep at home. On her desk was a list of absent students from the middle school, their contact information, and a note from the principal saying that she didn't think any of the absent students were arsonists. The note also mentioned that each homeroom teacher read a statement explaining what had happened and requesting any information that students may have.

Karen waited for Chief Reyes to get off the phone and then went to report what she'd found.

"It sounds like a pretty lame attempt at arson, like it was maybe some kids."

Karen shrugged. "Probably. Hopefully somebody will say something. The arsonist could have a bad burn that they're hiding."

TWENTY-FIVE

June 2021—Saratoga Springs, New York

Gil was bored with convalescence. He was still sore, it hurt to breathe, and his arm was still in a sling. He reluctantly decided to check out the senior center in town, something he didn't think he'd do until he was much older. Surprisingly, the parking lot was full, so he found a spot on the adjacent street.

The place was alive with activity. Everyone wore COVID masks of varying types, and modern music played in the background. In a large open area, staff were setting up chairs for a presentation. At one of several round tables, a group of rambunctious ladies was making rugs. A quieter group focused on cross-stitching at another table. People walked to and fro, and Gil heard the sounds of singing and ukuleles from another room.

A middle-aged woman came up to Gil. "Hi, I'm Caroline. Do you need some help?"

Gil stopped trying to make out the words being sung. "Well, I recently retired, so I thought I'd check this place out. My name is Gil."

"Well, Gil, you look like you had an accident!"

"Yes I did. I took a look at your website, but could someone show me around?"

"I'll show you around. This is the main hall where we're setting up for a speaker who's talking about Alzheimer's disease at eleven thirty. It's being presented remotely, and some people will join from home instead of risking COVID exposure. You can probably tell, but a lot goes on here. We're trying to get more men involved in meetings, but the guys tend to have hobbies that don't lend themselves to meeting here as a group. These people over there are having a chit-chat session facilitated by an intern from Skidmore College." To Gil, the people in the chit-chat seemed very old and needed encouragement to interact.

Caroline led Gil down a corridor. "As you can see, we have rooms for learning music, activities involving computers, and activities requiring smaller meeting rooms. Here we have a great kitchen for preparing meal events, but we haven't been doing that much lately thanks to COVID. There is a barbecue coming up soon, now that the warm weather is here. We also prepare food for Meals on Wheels, if you're interested in volunteer activities. Any particular interests bring you here?"

"I'm just figuring out what's available. I was doing some outside activities, but then I got injured, so I've been a little bored."

"Here's our latest newsletter, which you can also read on our website. It costs twenty-five dollars to join the Senior Center. would you like to join?"

"Sure, why not." Caroline brought him over to the main desk and had him fill out a form. She entered his information into a computer and processed his payment.

"There you go, Gil. You'll get all the information you need in your email since that's the preference you selected."

"Thanks, Caroline. I'll just hang around a little more and get a feel for the place."

Gil walked over to the music class and watched them through the large hallway windows. The musicians-to-be seemed to be having fun, even though most of them weren't playing very well. In the next room, Gil watched an art class where everyone was painting a picture of a butterfly clinging to a flower. The people in that room seemed to be deeply focused on their work. The pictures he could see were very different versions of the sample at the front of the room, but they were good all the same.

As Gil made his way back toward the front door, someone turned up the background music. "Achy Breaky Heart" was playing. The women from the rug-making and cross-stitching tables all got up and immediately arranged themselves to start line dancing. One woman was curling her finger toward Gil, trying to get him onto the dance floor. One woman from the chit-chat group was enthusiastically clapping to the music, so Gil went over and asked her to dance. She nodded, so Gil took off his sling, unlatched her wheelchair, and wheeled her onto the dancing line.

He didn't know how to line dance, but he did his best to gyrate and move the wheelchair around with the dancers. People clapped when the dance finished. An intern came over and told Gil that Blanche would be talking about that dance for a long, long time. Blanche was thrilled.

As he drove home, Gil decided that he'd be comfortable going back to the senior center to listen to a lecture or participate in a class again, if he felt the need for interaction. His shoulder and hip were sore, though.

———————

The next day, Gil went to Soave Faire, the art supplies store in town. The painting supplies were way in the back, and a guy back there was stocking shelves. "Excuse me, I wonder if I can get some help with painting supplies. I would like to try my hand at painting."

The guy looked at Gil's sling and said, "Well, I hope you're not using that hand. Do you want watercolors, oils, or acrylics?"

"Not watercolors. What's the difference between oils and acrylics?"

"Acrylics are easier for a beginner, and a lot of the pros prefer them."

"Okay, acrylics."

The guy gathered a set of paints, brushes, canvases, an easel, and other accessories, then brought them to the checkout counter. "I recommend two things to start: find a YouTube instructor you like, and paint from a photo, not from real life."

When Gil got home, he spread out his art supplies on the dining room table. He grabbed a pomegranate seltzer and started sampling YouTube's painting-instruction videos for acrylics. There were a lot of them. In some, the instructor didn't explain things sufficiently; in others, the instructor's voice or mannerisms annoyed him. A lot of them had no voice at all, just background mood music. Mostly, the instructor had you paint a specific picture along with them.

Gil chose an instructor with a pleasant voice who would paint some flowers while explaining the process. Gil set up his easel in his basement workshop. The instructor only needed ten minutes to paint, but Gil needed an hour and a half. In the end, Gil's painting had a few flaws, but it actually came out pretty good, including the one flower that looked a bit like a titmouse. He felt relaxed rather than stressed during the process, which was a key test for this activity. He learned a lot, and he decided to try a few more instructor videos before painting on his own. Then he had a better idea.

───────────

Gil eased his car into the parking garage across from the library. He walked over to Henry Street and found the Saratoga Paint and Sip Studio. The instructor looked like a college girl. She handed Gil an apron and welcomed him to get a drink from the bar. He hesitated, but then decided to get himself a glass of merlot. He found a seat among a dozen women and schoolgirls. Surprisingly, he didn't feel embarrassed that he was the only guy.

Once everybody was settled, the instructor said, "Hi, I'm Charlie. Welcome to our Paint and Sip session. Please remember, it's sip, not gulp." People snickered. "This evening we're going to be painting this picture." The picture was a stylized tree surrounded by flowers and with an owl in it. It seemed like a Van Gogh–style painting to Gil, from what little he knew about art. "Everything you need is at your table. Your goal should be to paint your version of this picture, rather than a duplicate. I'll paint my version of it so you can follow the steps that I take. Before you start, please write your first names on your name cards.

"The canvases are already primed with gesso, so you don't have to bother with that step." She started by mixing some colors and painting a rolling landscape, followed by the sky. Gil painted along with the rest of the people. Everyone was focused and fairly quiet. Charlie then painted the big dark tree with curly branches. As the students attempted the tree, the rate of sipping and the noise level both picked up as people realized how different theirs looked from the original.

Charlie walked around the room, giving people hints to help them. Gil was diligent in estimating the size of each branch by visualizing the branches as wire bundles in a robotic mechanism. When the tree was done, they put the outline of the big owl on a branch. Then came the highlights and details. The older woman next to Gil told him she was Lynne and asked him his name. Gil told her his name and the child next to her elbowed her in the ribs and said, "Stop flirting, Gramma. Jeez!"

By the time they were putting on the final details, the group was at its most boisterous. Gil didn't notice the people having fun all around him; he was too focused on his painting. The acrylic paint dried fast, so when they were done, Charlie asked everyone to turn their paintings around for everyone to see. Gil thought most of them were very good, but a few were pretty horrible. Again, all different versions of the original, and the children seemed to make larger owls with more cartoon-like features.

"Gil, would you please bring your painting up here." Gil brought it up and handed it to Charlie. She placed it next to the original, and the others gave a collective *ooh*. She said, "Your picture is almost exactly like the original! Have you ever considered a career as an art forger?" A collective laugh rolled through the room.

TWENTY-SIX

June 2021 — Greenfield, Massachusetts

It was ten o'clock on a Saturday night when Karen got called about another apparent arson. She and Jeff were at a friend's house playing Pictionary after going out to dinner. Jeff dropped her off at Newton Elementary School with the firefighters at the back of the building. Chief LaFarge said, "This fire's a lot like the middle school fire last month. The arsonist broke that window, poured some gasoline, and threw a lit match inside. This time there was more damage inside because some paper and cloth caught fire, and it spread. There wasn't any fire outside the building.

"There's a surveillance camera over there," said Officer Jupe. "I called the principal, Judy Light, and she should be here soon."

"Who called it in?"

"Nobody," said LaFarge. "The fire alarm was triggered at nine thirteen, and we responded."

Jupe said, "There weren't any witnesses around when I got here either."

Police Chief Reyes arrived. He looked at Karen up and down because she was wearing her dress. "I feel underdressed. I must not have got the memo." Karen rolled her eyes and gave him an update. He just nodded, said, "Keep me informed," and left.

When Principal Light showed up a couple of minutes later, Karen and Chief LaFarge followed her in to inspect the damage. "It isn't too bad, really," said the principal. "Mostly superficial damage, and some of the bookcases will need to be replaced."

LaFarge pointed at the ground. "This is where it started, and there's the remnant of the match that started it."

"I'm going to get some Crime Scene techs up here in the morning," said Karen. "Officer Jupe, tape off the scene, inside and out. Principal Light, please show us the surveillance video."

As they walked up to the office, the principal said, "Please call me Judy."

"I'm Detective Tindall." Judy accessed the surveillance video on an office PC and let Karen scan it with Chief LaFarge looking over her shoulder. "There he is!" said Karen. "We had a fire at the middle school a few weeks ago, and we thought it was probably kids, but we didn't get any video. This shows a big guy, but he's in the shadows. I can't really see what he looks like. Please send me a copy of this, and I'll see if the techs can improve it. Also, please copy the video of the night before. He may have done some reconnaissance."

Karen met with Chief Reyes the next day at the station. She was frustrated. "The techs tried to improve the arson video, but it isn't good enough. All we know is that it's an adult, probably male. I checked surveillance from nearby businesses, but there's no sign of this guy. There isn't any other good evidence. The melted gas can from last month just showed oil and sawdust residue that says it was probably used for chain saws. I don't have a motive. The fires were lame and didn't really accomplish anything, but next time someone could get killed."

"What do you think we should do next?" Reyes asked.

"All I can think of is to put better surveillance cameras on all of the schools."

Reyes did a search on his computer. "I've sent you the website of a security company in Springfield. I know the owner, Garrett Lawrence, from the army. Tell him it's me asking and that you need it right away. You can coordinate with the school superintendent."

TWENTY-SEVEN

April 1971—Keeseville, New York

Deputy Loring had gone to the hospital with Jacqui in the back of the ambulance to stand guard. Whoever assaulted her wouldn't get to try again. Deputy LeBrun got his camera out of the cruiser and went to look for evidence. There wasn't much to see, except for the circle of blood where Jacqui was found. He took a picture of it, along with the surrounding area.

In the house, he searched around near the telephone and found an address book, which he took. As he was leaving, he noticed baby toys and a crib, so he checked the bedrooms and the cellar. There was evidence of an older kid too. Nancy, the dispatcher, called him on his radio. "Husband's name is Remi Foy. He's driving a 1962 Rambler station wagon, beige. I put out an all-points bulletin."

"Nancy, it looks like he's got a baby and another kid with him."

Nancy sighed. "Okay, I'll update the APB."

———————

When Deputy LeBrun got to the emergency room in Plattsburgh, his partner was talking to a couple of deputies from Clinton County. Loring said, "These guys are going to post a guard since we're in their territory. They already have the APB for Remi Foy."

Deputy Vance said, "Since this is domestic and the husband took off, I don't think we'll keep a guard for more than a day."

"Yeah, whatever the brass decides," said LeBrun. "What did the doctor say?"

"She's still unconscious," said Loring. "He's waiting for an X-ray of her head."

A nurse brought LeBrun a mug of coffee, as she had done for the others. He tipped his hat and thanked her. She beamed and wiggled her hips as she walked back to her station.

After a few minutes, Doctor Pelletier came out. "She's got a fractured skull and some bleeding in her brain. I've seen much worse people do okay after a while, but with the brain, you never know. I'll let you know when she wakes up."

Back at their station, LeBrun and Loring filled in Detective Art Wisniewski on what they knew. Wisniewski said, "It's a pretty straightforward domestic, but it gets tricky when kids are involved. I'll take the address book and see if I can find out where Foy's heading and see if we can get some family to Plattsburgh. You guys should talk to the neighbors to see if they heard any fighting."

Art started making calls. "Regina Foy? This is Detective Wisniewski with the Essex County Sheriff's Department. Are you related to a Remi Foy?"

"I'm his mother. What's he done this time?"

"I'm afraid it's pretty bad, ma'am. It looks like he got in a fight with his wife and put her in the hospital. She's in tough shape."

"What about the girls?"

"He took off with the girls, near as we can tell. We're trying to track them down and make sure they're okay. Have you seen them?"

"I haven't seen 'em for a few years. Me and Remi don't get along. He doesn't really get along with nobody. Poor Jacqui!"

"Could you tell me the names and ages of the girls, ma'am?"

"Let me think. Marie would be about sixteen, and Angela would be, um, about twelve."

"I'm sorry, ma'am. The deputies said there was evidence of a baby."

"Oh my, I don't know about a baby. I don't know what to think about that. Is Jacqui going to be okay?"

"The doctor doesn't know yet. It's touch and go. Does Remi have any family or friends that he would go to for help?"

"He has two older brothers and an older sister, but I'd be surprised if any of them would help him. Nobody gets along with Remi."

"Ma'am, do you know Jacqui's maiden name?"

"It's Laurent. Jacqui Laurent."

Art took down the siblings' names and addresses and thanked Mrs. Foy, promising to let her know when they find the children. He found one address book entry for the Laurents—Albert and Danielle, who lived in Saint-Jerome, Canada. He called the operator to make an international call. The phone rang and a woman said, "Bonjour."

"Um, do you speak English? Is this Danielle Laurent?"

"Yes, who is this?"

"This is Detective Wisniewski from the Essex County Sheriff's Department in New York. Do you know a Jacqui Foy, ma'am?"

"Ah, *oui*. Yes. She is my husband's sister. What is the matter? Is Jacqui okay?"

"I'm afraid she's been hurt. She's in the hospital in Plattsburgh in serious condition."

Art could hear Danielle talking to a man in the background, and he came on the phone, also speaking with a French accent. "This is Al Laurent, Jacqui's brother. What happened to my sister?"

"We're not entirely sure yet, but it looks like she was in a fight with her husband. She ended up in serious condition, and we're searching for Mr. Foy."

Although Art didn't know French, he could tell that Al was swearing under his breath. "What about the girls?"

"It looks like he may have taken them with him. There's a baby too."

"A baby?" He was speaking in French to Danielle in the background.

"Sir, is there a family member who can come to the hospital to be with Jacqui?"

"Yes, yes. We will come today."

TWENTY-EIGHT

August 2021—Saratoga Springs, New York

It was two months since his accident, and Gil finally felt ready to head back to Greenfield for a visit. He'd gone stir-crazy because of the limitations on his physical activity, so he was anxious to travel. Before leaving, Gil went to a morning appointment with his sleep doctor. Gil discussed the last couple of weeks from his sleep log with Dr. Manomoney.

"Still no problems falling asleep, I see. It seems that you are getting more deep sleep, but you are not sleeping very long—only about four and a half hours. How do you feel?"

"Well, I'm not waking up with nightmares anymore. It's amazing! I feel a lot better than I did. I don't get drowsy during the day, but I still struggle to stay awake in the evenings."

"What do you do when you wake up at three in the morning?"

"I lie in bed, hoping I'll fall asleep again."

She thought for a few seconds and said, "Okay, I want you to try making two changes. The first is that, instead of going to bed at eleven, I want you to go to bed at one. Do you think you can do that?"

"I'll have to do something that keeps me more awake at night. Reading and watching TV definitely are not working."

"People have had the most success with activities that use their hands, like knitting or doing puzzles. But as we discussed before, stay away from using blue screens for an hour before bedtime. Let me know what you come up with. The other thing I want you to do is, when you wake up before, say, six, if you can't get back to sleep within about twenty minutes, get out of bed and go do something else like reading in another room for about a half hour. Still no blue screens. Then go back to bed and see if you can fall asleep."

"I think I'm okay to drive in the afternoons now, but not at night. Can we relax my driving restriction?"

"Yes, I think it's reasonable for you to just restrict your driving to daytime. If daytime drowsiness becomes an issue, we'll have to go back to more restrictions."

This time, Gil took his motorcycle on a different route to Greenfield through Hoosic Falls, down to Williamstown, then east on the Mohawk Trail through North Adams. He headed up into the Berkshire Mountains, past the hairpin turn, then up to the Whitcomb Summit, where he stopped for a break. In the mountains, the August air was starting to smell a little bit like fall, and a few of the trees had tinges of red and yellow. Gil chatted with a couple who pulled in next to him on their Harley. Coincidentally, they were heading to Saratoga Springs to watch their granddaughter in a rowing regatta. Gil gave them some restaurant tips and headed on his way.

When Gil got to Greenfield, he headed right to the police station to see Karen, who was expecting him. She said, "Perfect timing. I just started to look at some DNA results. The DNA from the remains shows several genetic defects that were responsible for the severe abnormalities in the remains. They're consistent with the deceased child being the result of an incestuous relationship."

105

"Do you have any DNA samples from his family?"

"The lab couldn't get any DNA from the bullets, so they're checking the other stuff that was in the bin, the remnants of the child's clothing, and a few other items found in the cave back in the nineties."

"I read that paleoanthropologists can get DNA samples from the dirt in caves," said Gil. "They can even read the DNA from samples that are a hundred thousand years old, to some extent. Maybe we can get one of those scientists to help the crime lab."

"Huh." Karen wrote a note on a pad by her computer. "I'll ask Lili about that. Where did you read that?"

"I read it in *New Scientist* magazine, which is from the UK. It comes every week."

She said, "So you're a science nerd! You don't strike me as being overly nerdy."

"Thanks, I think. What else did you get?"

"Well, we tried to trace the rope that was used in your attempted murder, but it's a common product found in every hardware store. We're checking the rope for DNA. Oh, and I did interview Ms. Florakis in New Hampshire. The main thing I found out is that New Castle, New Hampshire is absolutely gorgeous, and I want to live there. Anyway, she said that she vaguely remembered the family with the very young mom, but that they came in for a night or two and went right back out. She said that in the early years, their commune, the Leverett Farm, was somewhat militant and sabotaged anything and everything associated with the siting of a proposed nuclear plant. It wasn't a safe place for children."

"What did Ms. Florakis do after the commune?" Gil asked.

"Oh, she's a realtor, but she's also been involved with environmental activist groups, like Greenpeace, the Sierra Club—those kinds of groups. That's why she was reluctant to talk to the police. She's seventy-eight and still working! That's about all I have. Oh, I tried to track down Seth Wheeler, Astral Plane's head of security, but he died of natural causes years ago. To tell you the truth, since you were injured, I've been tied up with several new cases including an embezzlement and a couple of arsons."

"That's not good. What kind of places are being burned?"

"A couple of schools in town, hardly any damage. One in June and one in July. We got a glimpse of the arsonist on surveillance cameras but no clear picture. It looked like an adult or older teenager. It might be a pyromaniac. Anyway, what do you think we should do next on the cold case? I like your idea about DNA from the cave dirt. If we do that, I should get a DNA sample from you since we were in the cave recently."

Gil thought about it for a few seconds. "Sure, no problem."

Gil looked at some crime scene pictures of a fire-damaged school room on Karen's desk. "What if these fires are connected to our case?"

"You mean a diversion?"

"Well yeah, they could be intentionally distracting you from working on the cold case."

They wandered over to the chief's office, and Karen told Reyes about Gil's thought about the arson case. He smiled, gave him a sideways glance, and said, "So far, that's the only idea that fits. People told me you were a smart son-of-a bitch. Thanks for coming back."

Gil smiled back. "Thanks for fixing my bike."

TWENTY-NINE

April 1971—Greenfield, Massachusetts

After about a mile of walking, Remi and the kids reached a little country store called Harper's, and they bought some snacks while Remi asked for directions. Outside, Angela shared a blue ice pop with Julian. He squealed with delight, and both their mouths turned blue. When they got going again, they turned down another road and found the town's public swimming pool. It wasn't open for the summer yet, but they decided to explore. Several small sand beaches were set on a riverbank and there was a concession building. A footbridge to the other side of the river led to some picnic tables and grills.

"This is nice!" said Marie. "Maybe we could stay in Greenfield a while."

Remi walked over to a group of hippies who were smoking and drinking under some huge weeping willow trees by the water. They had loud music playing on a tape player, and a couple of girls were dancing. "Hey, do you guys know where I can find a gas station around here?" he asked.

A white guy with a huge Afro smiled and said, "Sure! Go up that way to the end of this road, take a right and a left, and keep going. It's maybe a mile. Want to join us?"

"No thanks, I'm good." He saw that Marie and Angela had joined the hippy girls in dancing to the music while holding Julian and Theo. Remi felt anger rising up in his neck, and he growled. "Let's go now." He didn't like music. He didn't trust it.

Just as Afro Guy said, after about a mile they reached a Sunoco station, so Remi went inside, described his problem to the owner, and signed a work order to tow the car and take a look at it. Remi asked about restaurants, and the gas station owner suggested a few nearby choices. They continued walking until they found the A&W restaurant.

While they were sitting at a picnic table eating food and drinking root beer, Marie saw a line of boys on ramshackle bicycles come flying down the hill behind the restaurant, each skidding to a stop. While they ordered food, she walked over and asked one of them, "Hey, where did you guys just come from on your bikes?"

"Poet's Seat. We rode the trail back here. It's wicked!"

"We're not from around here. What's up there?"

"There's a stone tower, but the rest of it's just woods."

Marie went back to the table and told Remi what she learned. "Maybe we can go up that trail and make a camp."

After they ate, they walked up the narrow dirt path on the forested hill. There were many different types of trees, but their leaves hadn't yet fully emerged. As they went on, the trail skirted the edge of a cliff, which made them a little nervous. They found the tower and went up it, climbing a series of stone staircases. Near the top, a narrow, black-metal spiral staircase led to the top floor. That made them nervous, but they braved the climb all the way up.

Marie's face lit up. "We can see the whole town!" They took their time looking around, but when the baby started fussing, they decided to head down to the base of the tower.

Marie found a rock outcropping and started to feed Theo while Angela made sure Julian didn't fall down the cliff.

"You stay here," Remi said. "I'll go see if there's a place for us to camp."

About an hour later, Remi led them down the road and into the woods to a small cave. He then walked all the way back to the gas station, where his car was sitting outside the bay.

"I'm afraid your car is shot," the station owner said. "The engine is seized. It's scrap."

Remi was shocked. He asked, "What should I do?"

"Well, you owe me eighteen dollars for the tow, but I can sell the car for scrap. So, just get your stuff out of the car, and we'll call it even. Do you want your plates?"

Remi thought that without his car and license plates, it would be impossible for the police to find them. "Yeah, I'll take the plates. It'll take me a couple of trips to empty the car. Thanks for your help."

After making another trip with Marie to get the rest of their stuff out of the car, Remi went to get rope, more blankets, and tarps to set up a camp. It didn't take them long to fall asleep once the sun went down.

––––––––––––––

The next day, Remi brought the kids to a Grand Union supermarket for supplies. Every time he ran into a group of hippies, he engaged them and asked about where they were headed. After they got back to their campsite and had some lunch, the girls walked downhill to the bank of the Connecticut River to bathe. The water looked dark and deep and was rushing by very fast, so they decided it wasn't safe to wade in. Marie instead asked her father to get some buckets and rope so they could draw water.

After the sun went down, Marie was able to use their new battery-powered lantern to start a book called *The Black Pearl*, which she'd bought at the grocery store. The story took her away to a tropical paradise where a boy was diving for pearls. She was completely engrossed in the book when Angela screamed from the cave. Marie ran into the cave to find Angela half-naked and furiously kicking at her father, who had lowered his pants. Marie hit him in his right ear, which caused him to spin around, enraged. "You get out of here, right now!" yelled Marie. "You've already ruined me, and you will not touch her!"

He pulled up his pants with a scowl on his face. "You know, Marie, you're getting to look too much like your mother. But Angela's becoming quite a beauty." Marie hit him in the face with the heel of her hand and heard a crunch. He gagged, and his nose started gushing blood. Marie kicked him toward the cave entrance, and he stumbled out. Marie ran over and hugged Angela who was shaking with fear. "This will be over soon, Angel. Don't you worry." Marie helped Angela get her panties and pants back on and comforted her, knowing all too well how she felt.

THIRTY

Karen and Gil were sitting in a classroom at the Farnum Community School. Principal Donna Karpinsky and the admin assistant, Barb Bell, were rummaging through a box of files labeled "1971–1972." Everybody was wearing COVID masks—some cloth, some disposable.

Karen closed yet another folder. "We aren't sure she was even here, and we don't know what name she would have been registered under. If she was here, she would have been in about sixth or seventh grade, maybe."

Donna said, "We pulled the records from here, the middle school, and the commune school. We keep them in a warehouse downtown."

There was a knock on the door, and a woman in her seventies came in. "Hi Carole!" said Barb. "Everybody, this is Carole Newly. She was a teacher here back in the early seventies, and I thought she might be able to help. Carole, please put your mask up over your nose. It doesn't work unless you do that." Carole gave a sheepish look and complied.

Donna motioned for Carole to sit. "This is exciting," said Carole. "Like *Law and Order*! I'm not sure I'll be much help, but I can tell you what it was like back then." She lowered her mask, took a big gulp from her water bottle, smacked her lips, wiped her mouth with the back of her hand, then put her mask back up. "Back then, I was teaching ninth- and tenth-grade English. In the early seventies, the commune started up their own school. Since they weren't accredited or anything, it was officially considered homeschooling, but they actually had some good, experienced schoolteachers create the curriculum and teach the students. The students got all the normal subjects, but they had a lot more music and art, and also the commune's version of religious studies."

"Religious studies?" Gil asked.

"Well, I think they considered what they had as a kind of spiritualism rather than a religion. It combined some aspects of Buddhism and Hinduism. Some mysticism too.

"After a few years, we started to get some of the hippy children. We ended up with quite a lot of them over the years. They were poor, dirty, and smelly, but some of them were wicked smart. Their parents seemed that way too. They could have been stockbrokers or lawyers, but most of them just chose to work on a farm for a while. Anyway, we weren't ever confident that their identities were valid, but the superintendent convinced the school board that the kids needed to be schooled regardless of whoever they were."

"Why didn't you believe their identities?" asked Karen.

"Some of them had names that sounded made up, both the parents and the kids. The hippy movement hadn't been around for very long, so it seemed like they invented those names just before showing up. You know, instead of Jane, you had Jasmine, and instead of Joe, you had Josiah."

Gil asked, "What did you think about the last names they gave?"

"Some of them seemed fake too, but it didn't matter. We used whatever names they gave us. Most of them were from other parts of the country. You could tell by their accents and their different worldviews. A lot of them were from New York City and New Jersey."

"These boxes have the records from the commune's homeschool program," said Donna. "Here are the class pictures from the sixth and seventh grade." She handed them to Karen and Gil.

Gil put his reading glasses on and looked them over. "Ha, I suppose this could be her!" He looked at the list of names at the bottom. "This says the girl's name was Angel Forest. That definitely sounds made up."

"Why do you think it's a made-up name?" Karen asked.

"Back then, I never heard of any girl named Angel. Also, whenever I've seen that last name, it has two *r*'s but this has only one."

Barb rummaged around and said, "Here's her record. Her registration gives an address on Kingsbury Road, which was definitely the commune. It says she started on May 11, 1971."

"Can I borrow this picture?" Karen asked. "I'll send it back." Donna nodded. "Also, could you fax me a copy of the record?"

As they were walking out, Gil smiled at Karen. "Angel Forest could have been the angel in my nightmares."

———————

They had the windows down while they rode back to Greenfield, so they didn't feel the need to wear their masks. Karen's phone rang, and she answered it through the car's audio system. A woman said, "Detective Tindall, this is Terry

Billings. You questioned me and my husband a few weeks ago about a hippie family?"

"Hi, Terry. Of course, I remember you. I'm driving in a car with Gil Novak here too. What's up?"

"Well, I talked about your investigation on the Astral Plane Facebook page a while back. There was a little back-and-forth about how interesting that was. A few people remembered a little bit about it. But just last night, somebody said that they saw the family on Poet's Seat Mountain all those years ago, and there was a third child who was severely disabled. Was the child who died disabled in some way?"

Karen looked at Gil, whose face also showed excitement. "Well, I can't talk about the specifics of the investigation, but I can tell you that I'm really interested in contacting this person."

"So this could be a hot lead in a cold case! His name is Joel Friedman. I'll text you his number."

"Thank you so much, Terry. I really appreciate this." They ended the call.

Gil was piecing together the details. "So maybe a Facebook post could have been how the person who tried to kill me knew about this investigation."

———————————

They returned to the police station and Karen set up a Webex call with Joel Friedman in the conference room. "Hi, Mr. Friedman. I'm Detective Tindall with the Greenfield Police Department. Thank you for talking with us." Gil thought he looked like an executive.

"Please call me Joel."

"Okay, Joel. This is Gil Novak, who is assisting me with this investigation. We understand that you remember meeting a family up on Poet's Seat Mountain back in the seventies."

"Yes, that's correct." He chuckled. "I was a real hippie back then. A handful of us were hitchhiking and walking through Massachusetts, headed toward Farnum to check out the commune. At some point, this guy caught up to our group and asked us where we were headed. He was interested in checking out the communes too, but he was camping out with his kids and couldn't walk with us. As we were walking and talking, he offered to share some weed with us if we wanted to hike up a little mountain. Some girl and I took him up on his offer. You're not going to arrest me if I admit to smoking pot back then, are you?" He smiled.

Karen smiled. "Pot's legal in Massachusetts now, so you're okay. What was the girl's name?"

"Oh, I have no idea. I never really got to know her. Anyway, when we got to his campsite, I thought it was kind of cool because they were living in this cave. There were two girls there and one of them had a baby. We were passing around a joint, and all of a sudden, this deformed little kid showed up making an awful screeching noise. It couldn't walk, but it was sort of crawling around. It freaked us out, so we left."

"Did you ever see this family again?"

Joel thought for a minute and said, "I think I remember seeing the guy around the commune once or twice, but I never talked to him. I don't know his name or anything."

Gil moved closer to the webcam. "Where do you live, and what do you do for a living?"

"Oh, I retired a dozen years ago. I was a stockbroker for Ziegler in the city. Now I live in my beach house on Long Island and mostly on my sailboat in the winter. I usually sail down to the Virgin Islands. I'll be heading out next month."

"Nice!" Gil said. "One other thing, did you use your real name while at the commune?"

"Ha, no I didn't! My name was Rowan, Rowan Solus."

THIRTY-ONE

April 1971—Plattsburgh, New York

It was evening when Al and Danielle Laurent arrived at the hospital in Plattsburgh. After showing their licenses to the deputy in the corridor, a nurse took them to Jacqui's room. "She just opened her eyes a couple of hours ago," the nurse said, "but she hasn't said anything yet. I'll go get the doctor."

Doctor Pelletier came in and introduced himself. "Jacqui has a skull fracture and some bleeding in her brain. It's a very good sign that she opened her eyes, but she's not yet fully conscious. She did move her eyes a bit when I asked her to follow a flashlight, and she can move her finger when asked. These are good signs, but she's not out of the woods yet." Al and Danielle looked confused, so the doctor clarified. "We'll watch her overnight to see if she's getting better or not. It may help if you talk to her."

Detective Wisniewski stopped by and introduced himself. "It's good to see that Jacqui's eyes are open. I hope she recovers soon." He gave Danielle his card. "When she can talk, I'd like to find out more about what happened and where her husband may have gone. So far, we don't have any leads. Nobody has reported seeing Remi and the kids, and we don't have any information saying where they might have gone. We did find out that Remi was just fired from his job. It doesn't appear that his family would have helped him. They think he's trouble and don't talk to him. Like you, they didn't know there was a baby."

A nurse came in and asked if they would step out of the room for a few minutes. In the hallway, the detective said,

"We've booked you a hotel room, and we're paying for it. Also, here is some money for food."

"This is very kind of you," said Al. Thank you."

The next morning, Detective Wisniewski received a call from Al Laurent. Jacqui was talking, he said. The detective rushed to the hospital, but by then, Jacqui was sleeping. Al and Danielle were in the hallway drinking coffee from paper cups. Al shook his head and said, "Jacqui wakes up and then falls asleep. The doctor says it's due to the brain injury."

Danielle was quietly sobbing. "Jacqui said there are two babies, an infant and a two-year-old. She said they are Marie's children, and Remi is the father. She wants us to save her children."

Wisniewski was stunned.

"Jacqui said that the two-year-old has significant defects. He can't walk or speak, but he is healthy. His name is Julian."

Art wrote that down in his little notebook. "What about the infant?"

"She fell asleep before we could talk about the infant," Al said.

"Is there anything you need? Is your hotel okay?"

"We are fine. We just want you to catch Remi and make sure those kids are safe." The nurse came out. "Jacqui is awake again. You can go in."

"Mrs. Foy, I'm Detective Art Wisniewski with the Essex County Sheriff's Department. I'm working on finding your family and making sure the children are safe. Do you know where they might have gone?"

"No," she whispered. "They could be anywhere. Please save my girls!" Her voice was breathy but firm in conviction.

"Do you have any reason to think your husband would hurt the children?"

"He raped Marie and forces her to live as his wife. Angela will be next."

Art paused to consider the potential danger to Angela. "What about the babies?"

"Oh no, he loves those bastards." Danielle looked away, clearly disturbed by what Jacqui said.

"Could you tell me the name and age of the infant?"

"That's Theo. He's about a month old." Jacqui dozed off again.

THIRTY-TWO

August 2021—Greenfield, Massachusetts

Gil was crawling through a jungle, his knees bloodied by sticks and stones. A snake reared up and lunged at him, but he rolled away just in time. His eyes were stinging from sweat and blood, but he could just make out a clearing up ahead. He quickened his pace, then heard a roar immediately behind him. The tiger leaped at him, its teeth heading for his throat.

Gil woke up drenched in sweat, confused about where he was. It was pitch black except for a few blue and red LEDs, and he quickly realized that he was in his hotel room. He sat up on the side of the bed, his head pounding. A wave of nausea hit him, and he fumbled his way to the bathroom. A splash of cold water on his face helped him start to feel better.

It was 2:30 a.m., but he knew it would be a while before he could sleep again. He turned on a floor lamp by the reading chair, found his Kindle, and continued his novel about World War II in France. After a half hour, he felt tired enough to fall asleep.

When he woke up again, he could see the dim light of dawn through a gap in the drapes. He got up and went down to breakfast, but he didn't trust his stomach. It was early, and the breakfast area wasn't crowded. He sat down with a cup of decaf coffee and started reading the news on his cell phone. A young guy in a maroon, company-labeled polo shirt came into the breakfast area coughing. Everyone, including Gil, left the breakfast area to avoid getting COVID. A middle-aged couple went over and complained to the desk clerk. Gil went back to his room to finish his coffee.

———————————

Karen had a concerned look on her face. "Gil, based on some confusion with our DNA findings, we have a few questions for you. For these questions, I'll need to read you your rights."

Gil looked confused.

Karen led Gil to Chief Reyes's office. "We're going to record this conversation." Chief Reyes switched on a recording device on his desk. Karen stated Gil's name and the date and time, then read him the Miranda warning and asked, "Do you wish to have an attorney present?"

Gil thought about it. "No, I don't think I need one. I'm intrigued! Go ahead and ask your questions."

"During the DNA testing of the deceased child, we found your DNA on the remains. They've been sealed in a plastic bin since the early 1990s. Do you know how that could be?"

Gil chortled and thought for a minute. "I have no idea how that could possibly be. Maybe cross-contamination?"

"We thought of that possibility and ruled it out. Other possibilities are that you came in contact with the child in 1971 or something that had your DNA came in contact with the child before or after his death. Did you ever come in contact with that child?"

"No," Gil said definitively.

"Could the child have come in contact with something that had your DNA?"

"I really don't remember any details about what happened back then. I don't remember leaving anything behind, but I couldn't know for sure. What I think happened is that I fell, hit my head on some rocks, and when I came to, my head was bleeding. I suppose it's possible that the child or his family came in contact with my DNA that way."

Karen looked at Chief Reyes, and he gave a nod. Karen continued, "Thank you, Mr. Novak. This concludes the interview with Gil Novak. Gil, please step out of the office for a few minutes."

When he left, Karen said, "I think his explanation is the most plausible. I can't think of a reason why he'd come here out of the blue if he were guilty of something."

Chief Reyes motioned for Karen to bring him back in. "I'm sorry, Gil, but we've been following protocol here. We just discussed several reasons for this finding, but the least likely is that you had something to do with that child's death. I think your explanation of blood contact is probably the most likely explanation. I'd like you to continue helping Detective Tindall with her case." Gil nodded.

———————

Karen drove Gil back up to Poet's Seat Mountain, and they parked in the little parking area by the gate. "You know, this is officially called Rocky Mountain."

"What?" Gil asked.

"This mountain we all call Poet's Seat is officially named Rocky Mountain. Mountains are older than towers after all, and that's what this one was—and is supposed to be—called."

"Huh. Well, let's rename the mountain to what everybody calls it. You basically could call any mountain Rocky Mountain, and I seem to recall that a lot of the mountains in this country have that name."

She chuckled. "I'll put that on my to-do list."

When they got to the cave, a handful of young people were working around a grid of string all over the cave area. The glow of work lights lit up the cave. A man and a woman came up to them. "Gil Novak, this is Dr. D'Amico from the State Police Crime Lab."

"Please call me Lili." They nodded at each other in a proper social-distancing way. Lili was petite and very pretty. She was probably in her fifties but somehow seemed much younger. He felt himself blushing. "This is Dr. Flores from the UMass Department of Anthropology. Danny, this is Detective Tindall from the Greenfield Police Department."

"Gil Novak is my consultant," said Karen. "He saw the family who was camping in this cave back in 1971. He was also the one who suggested we contact UMass to look for DNA in the dirt. Lili has our DNA elimination samples."

Danny looked at Gil. "How did you know about our work in this area?"

"I didn't know specifically about this work at UMass, but I've read a lot about recent successes reading ancient DNA from dirt samples in caves from tens of thousands of years ago. I figured that you could probably find something from the seventies. I read about it in *New Scientist* magazine."

"I love that magazine!" Danny said.

"I've never heard of it," said Lili.

"It's from the UK."

"Well, Gil," said Danny, "as you can see, my team staked out the area, and we're taking samples in each grid location, layer by layer. We'll carbon-date biological material from each layer and analyze it for human DNA. The fact that the child's remains were exhumed from one area of the cave will complicate things a little because it mixed up the layers of soil, but we'll figure something out. This will take a week or so of fieldwork and two or three weeks for preliminary lab analysis."

Karen smirked. "Huh, that's much quicker than the crime lab, *Lili*."

"Hey, watch it. We're busy with a huge backlog, and everybody's samples are first priority. So Gil, what kind of guy reads British science magazines?"

"Hey, I do it to attract the ladies," said Gil. Everyone burst out laughing. "Actually, before I retired I spent a couple of years in the UK for work, and I picked up the magazine then."

"My consultant is worldly, it seems," said Karen. "Danny, why don't you show Gil your setup while I talk to Lili?" She grabbed Lili and steered her away. Gil could only hear bits and pieces of their conversation, but Karen was telling Lili about Cynthia's death.

"You know, Lili's single," Karen said on the drive back. "And she's a good friend of mine."

Gil thought for a moment. "I only talked to her for a few minutes, but I do find her interesting. It scares me a little." Karen glanced at him, and Gil had a sheepish look on his face.

"I'll give you her number if you promise to behave. By the way, Danny suggested that we check ourselves for ticks. He said they've seen a lot of 'em."

Gil grunted an acknowledgment, but his mind was busy sorting through his instant interest in a woman he didn't know and his lifelong commitment to Cynthia.

THIRTY-THREE

May 1971—Greenfield, Massachusetts

Remi had bought a little .22 caliber rifle and some bullets to hunt rabbits. So far, he'd only killed a couple of squirrels with the rifle, but they were edible in a stew that Marie made. He'd found a metal pipe sticking out of the mountain on the road toward Turner's Falls, and out of it gushed fresh spring water. Every day or two, Marie or Angela would go to the pipe and fill some milk jugs with water. They were doing okay camping, but the bugs were horrible.

While at the camp taking a break from hunting, he said, "We're running out of money, and it's too hard living like this. We're going to have to move. I'll need to get a job, and we can get a house. We'll need new names so the police don't come after us, so I think we should be the Forest family since we live in the woods. I'll be Luke. What do you want to be called?"

"Can I be Angel?" Angela asked.

"That's good," Remi said. "Angel's good."

"I'll be Willow," said Marie.

"Willow, okay. What about Julian?"

"Jules," Marie said. "We'll just call him Jules like we always have."

Remi nodded. "We can just call Theo 'Theo' since nobody even knows about him."

———————

During the next couple of weeks, "Luke" searched around town for a decent job, without much luck. Since Luke Forest didn't have a Social Security number, he'd have to work for cash. He hitchhiked over the river to Turner's Falls, but he still didn't find anything good enough. The communes were his best bet. The hippies told Luke they didn't get paid more than a little spending money, though they received room and meals. Luke thought that sounded kind of risky—he wanted anonymity—but perhaps he and the kids could just go there for a little while and leave if they needed to.

Back at the camp, Luke said, "Start packing up while I finish hunting. We're going to leave tomorrow." He hunted close to the riverbank where he'd shot a rabbit several days before. He shot two more squirrels, dressed them, and headed back up to camp. Luke was worried about getting used to their new names, including his own.

As he trudged up the hill, he thought he saw some movement beyond the camp. He stood still, spotting someone watching Willow from above. Luke put down the squirrels and shot twice just below the rise where the watcher had concealed himself. The watcher jumped up and started scrambling up the hill. Luke yelled to the girls, "Someone's spying on us! Get your stuff and head down the Indian path to the bridge. I'll chase him off."

"We can't carry the kids and all this stuff!" Marie—Willow—said.

"I'll take care of Jules. GO!"

He darted up the hill and shot a few more times near the feet of the intruder. The watcher looked like a teenage boy. The boy fell down hard onto his face and stopped moving. Luke panicked. Had he shot him? Luke approached cautiously, then nudged the boy with his foot. He didn't move. Hopefully he was just knocked out or playing dead. Luke kicked him onto his back and winced. The boy's face was covered in blood that streamed from a gash on his head. He hadn't been shot, but he was definitely out cold. Luke was relieved, but then another thought hit him. What if the boy wasn't alone? The others would have heard the gunshots.

Luke ran back down to the campsite and grabbed his stuff together and looked around for anything else he should take. He heard Jules screeching outside, so he went out to grab him. Jules was up the hill, climbing onto the head of the boy. Luke screamed in panic,"Jules, get off! Get off! As Luke ran up to get him, the boy woke up, screaming and flailing. Jules was thrown against a tree. The boy got up and stumbled up the hill, probably blinded by the blood in his eyes.

Jules was hurt! Luke picked him up, and Jules twitched in his arms. Then he went still. His neck was broken. Luke let out a primal scream and started sobbing. His son was dead, and someone would definitely be coming for him. He ran to the cave, desperately dug a shallow grave using a stick and his hands, and buried Jules. He carefully tamped the soil back down so nobody would see it. It was all he could do. He grabbed his stuff and took off down the road after tossing his rifle into a thicket.

THIRTY-FOUR

September 2021—Saratoga Springs, New York

Gil had been back in Saratoga for a couple of weeks. Karen said she'd call him when she needed him again. He was in for another session with Dr. Manomoney, who was looking at his sleep log. "You were doing much better, but it seems like the past couple of weeks have been more difficult. What's going on?"

"I started to have nightmares again. Sometimes they're the worst I've ever had. I probably need to go see Dr. Lipton again."

"Let's make that happen as soon as possible. Remember, good sleep is about establishing a pattern of good sleep behaviors. We don't want these nightmares to root themselves in your sleep pattern again."

———————————

Dr. Lipton couldn't take him for two weeks. In the meantime, Gil was back at pickleball, frustrated with his serves. One of the experienced players, who looked to be about eighty, asked him if he'd like some help. Gil told the guy about his motorcycle accident and recovery. The guy gave him some tips on how to get his serve back. "Don't toss the ball up to serve," he said. "Just let it drop as your paddle is coming up." Gil followed his advice, and pretty soon he was serving in bounds, most of the time. After the last game of the day, the pickleball organizers debated whether to move the game indoors to the YMCA. They decided that, due to COVID, they would keep playing outside until the weather got too cold or snowy. Gil decided that he wouldn't play indoors until there was very little COVID around. He wouldn't feel comfortable playing pickleball wearing a mask.

When he checked his phone, he had a text from Karen: "Call me." He gave her a buzz.

"We got DNA results from the cave," she said. "We have DNA from four other family members."

"Four?"

"A male, two females who are the children of the male, and another child which was also conceived incestuously by the father and one of the daughters. The lab also picked up our DNA and the DNA of quite a few other unknown people. They also got DNA from a variety of animals, unsurprisingly. The UMass team separated the DNA in time by dating the layers of soil. They dated the surface layers for us, including the child's grave, which was about a foot and a half deep. They went even deeper for their own research into Indigenous peoples and extinct animal DNA. They'll be analyzing those samples for a while. They said people were living in this area when the glaciers receded around fourteen thousand years ago."

"Wow, fourteen thousand years! I had no idea. So what do we do next?"

"Lili's going to work with a forensic genealogist to see if we can find some family members. Maybe that'll give us some leads."

"This is really cool. Let me know when you want me to come back."

"It may be a while," said Karen. "I've got those arsons going on, and if they're related to our case, I don't want to put you in harm's way again. We're up to four arsons now. One a month."

THIRTY-FIVE

May 1971—Greenfield, Massachusetts

As Willow and Angel hurried down the mountain, Willow thought about taking off. They could take the trail to Bear's Den or the road toward Deerfield, but Willow couldn't leave Jules behind. They headed over the bridge to Turner's Falls and stopped on the other side to wait for their father and Jules.

It seemed to take forever. When Luke finally showed up, he was alone and crying. "Julian is dead! He's dead! It was an accident."

Angel burst into tears. Willow yelled, "You bastard! What did you do with him?"

"I buried him in the cave. The boy who was watching you took off, and he was hurt. The cops will be after us. Let's go. We're going to the commune."

They hitchhiked into Turner's Falls where they bought food with some of the last of their money. They continued to hitchhike through rural, forested lands, crossing bridges over rivers and brooks. At the turnoff to Farnum, they camped in the woods by a pond. All of them were angry and upset, but nobody said anything.

The next day they walked some more, eventually joining up with a group of hippies who were also headed to the commune. Upon arriving, they were directed to an office in the front room of an old farmhouse. A woman in her early twenties came out to talk to the group on the front porch. She put her hands together, bowed her head, said namaste, then waited expectantly. The newcomers looked at each other and realized they should respond in kind, which they did awkwardly.

"Namaste is a traditional Hindu greeting from India that means 'I bow to you.' Here at the Astral Plane Commune, you'll be expected to participate in our spiritual journey, which is an essential part of our community. My name is Summer. For the first two weeks, you'll be considered prospective members. During this time, you'll participate in the work of the community, wherever you are assigned. You'll also be expected to attend meetings and meditations. For these two weeks, you'll learn what we're all about, and we'll also decide if you're a good fit for us. At the end of the two weeks, if you want to stay, and if Vincent, our leader, wants you to stay, you will give up all of your money and worldly possessions of value to the commune, including your cars. You'll pledge to support our community and abide by our rules. Our rules include no alcohol, no drugs, and no promiscuity."

A few guys chuckled. Theo started to cry, embarrassing Willow, but Summer just smiled at her.

"Are there any questions?"

After they all registered, Summer showed them to a huge plastic tent that smelled like sweat and dirty laundry. This would be the living area for all prospective members for the next two weeks. Summer showed them the outhouse and where they could get water. At the dining hall, they shared a meal of rice and beans.

In the evening, everybody was invited to a meeting outside the dining hall. Luke, Willow, and Angel sat on the grass among the commune members. Theo was asleep in Willow's arms. Vincent, the commune's leader, stepped onto the small stage and gave a little bow with his hands together. "Namaste!" he said, and the crowd returned the greeting. "I'm happy to see our community is thriving and growing. Over the past year, I have traveled the country and witnessed earthly changes that are transforming our world. Young people like us are rebelling against wars, prejudice, and corruption. We are forming an entirely new culture! Our commune is a beacon of light in the darkness. Together, we are again learning what the ancients had already known about humanity. My own writings will help the world understand these truths."

An acoustic band got up on stage and started to play "For the Times They Are A-Changin'." Audience members got up and started to dance, including Willow and Angel, who rested Theo on the ground. They moved with the rhythm of the music and were entranced by the sounds, lyrics, and motions. Luke felt anxious around the music and the dancing, but he didn't want to make a scene. He wanted to hear more about ancient knowledge and earthly changes.

In the morning, Luke suggested that the girls go to the bathroom together. "It's an outhouse with two holes. A strange man could be sitting next to you while your pants are pulled down."

While they were in the dining hall eating a breakfast of oatmeal, a young man named Trevor asked Luke to come with him to join the logging crew. During registration, Luke indicated that he had experience in logging and working in lumber mills. Trevor showed Luke where they were starting to clear several acres of woodland to build more buildings. When Luke saw how young all the men were and how they were working, he said, "The way you're doing this is very inefficient and unsafe. It'll take too many people and too much time." The people loggers were using hatchets and very small chainsaws. They were pulling logs up the hill manually with ropes. They also didn't have any safety gear except work gloves.

"The commune doesn't have much money," Trevor said.

"Time is money. Here is what I think you should do. Get some twenty-four- and thirty-six-inch chainsaws for taking down trees and limbing. I've seen a lot of guys get seriously injured doing this kind of work. Everyone should be wearing hard hats, goggles, and steel-toed boots. They also should have wedges for the cuts to prevent kickbacks. We can make wedges from wood. To haul the logs up the hill, you'll need a machine with chains instead of ropes, either a skidder or a hoist." He thought about it for a few seconds and asked, "Do you have a tractor?"

Trevor seemed overwhelmed. "Um, maybe we could borrow one?"

"Good, show me your sawmill." Trevor was flustered. He was just supposed to be putting Luke to work, but he clearly had someone who knew what they should be doing. He just nodded and led Luke up the hill.

A woman named April brought Willow and Angel to the nursery school, which had about ten children and three infants. Willow settled Theo into an old crib, and Angel went to play with the toddlers. April told Willow, "Dina should be here in a few minutes. When she comes, I'll take Angel over to the school. Here we have school even in summer so the parents are free to work."

"I should come with you to take Angel to the school," Willow said. "She's been anxious since her mom died recently." Willow went over to Angel, put her arm around her, and whispered that she would come with her to the school and that she'll visit her throughout the day. At first, Angel seemed agitated, but then she settled down. When Dina arrived, April walked Willow and Angel over to a dusty barn, which had been divided up into several rooms with makeshift walls, each room for a different age group.

"Our school teaches all of the normal subjects, but Vincent has them focus specially on effective speaking and writing. The kids also get classes on spirituality. What grade are you in, Angel?"

Angel looked at Willow, confused. Willow said, "She was finishing up sixth grade when we left home."

April brought Angel over to the seventh- and eighth-grade classroom and introduced her to the teacher, Rena. She took Rena aside and whispered to her about the recent death of Angel's mom.

On the way back to the nursery school, April asked, "Are you and Angel sisters?"

"Yes."

"You look kind of young to have a baby."

"I'm older than I look."

At the end of a long workday, April brought them to Meditation. Most of the commune seemed to be assembling there as they sat down. Willow thought the other people looked very dirty, and she realized that she must look that way too. Angel huddled in next to her sister. A woman led the meditation, and the girls did their best to follow along. It was hard for them to relax in the unfamiliar situation, but the drone of the mantra, along with the freshening breeze and darkening sky, helped Willow relax. She snapped out of it and cringed when Luke sat down beside her.

THIRTY-SIX

September 2021—Saratoga Springs, New York

When Karen called, Gil was taking measurements to cut a piece of floor tile for the bathroom.

"Lili's got a hot lead for us. I'd like you to join a video conference with us. I'll send you a link."

When they were all connected, Lili said, "Hi, Gil. It's been a while. When will we be seeing you again?"

Gil felt a bit flustered in Lili's presence. "Um, I don't know. Karen's been too busy to invite me back to your area, I guess. Maybe I'll have to visit the Basketball Hall of Fame or something."

"Oh, do you follow basketball?"

"No, not at all."

Lili grinned. Karen did too. "I've been busy getting nowhere on my arsons, so maybe I'll invite you back pretty soon."

"Our forensic genealogist at UMass found a DNA match for a grandmother of the deceased child," said Lili. "Her name is Helene Faucher, and she lives in Saint-Jerome, Canada."

Gil lit up. "Holy moly! Have you talked to her?"

"We're making preparations to talk to her," said Karen. "Chief Reyes has to run it up the management chain first. Even the US State Department has to be notified. Once that's done, I'll contact the police up there and arrange a conference call. I would have liked to travel up there and talk to Helene in person, but COVID restrictions are making that too complicated."

Karen had Chief Reyes in the conference room, and Gil had joined the call from his home computer. Detective Alan Mason and Helene Faucher were in the police station in Sainte-Jerome and everyone introduced themselves. Detective Mason said, "Mademoiselle Faucher has been informed that the purpose of this meeting is to discuss the remains of a child discovered in 1991 in Massachusetts. DNA analysis shows him to be Miss Faucher's grandchild. I've explained Miss Faucher's rights, and she has declined to have a solicitor present."

"Very well," said Karen. "I'll get started. The child in question was a boy who died in about 1971. He was about two or three years old and had significant birth defects."

Helene sniffed back some tears. She had dark eyes and nicely cut salt-and-pepper hair. "That was Marie's baby, Julian. Do you know what happened to Marie and Angela?" Helene spoke with a French accent.

Karen began frantically taking notes. "Fantastic. Those are the names we've been looking for. Please, what are their last names?"

Helene had a hopeful look. "Foy. Marie and Angela Foy, my daughters."

"There was a man with them. Do you know his name?"

A darkness came over Helene's face. She looked at Detective Mason, then looked at the camera. "That's their father, Remi Foy. He took my daughters from me." A few more tears fell.

Karen waited for Helene to regain her composure. "Could you tell me what happened?"

"We were living in Keeseville, New York. Remi was my husband at the time. He beat me up, fractured my skull, then took my daughters and left." She started to cry harder. "I haven't heard from them since then. I'm sorry." They all stayed silent and let Helene cry for a few more moments. "Remi raped Marie. He only wanted young girls. He would have raped Angela next." She cried harder, then took a sip of tea from a ceramic mug. "I was afraid he would come back and kill me, so I moved back to Canada and changed my name. I divorced him for physical cruelty."

"What was your name, and what was the baby's name?" Karen asked.

"My name was Jacqui, Jacqui Foy." She spelled her first name. "Originally, I was Jacqui Laurent. The baby's name was Theo. There aren't any records of those two babies because they were born at home and were never, um, registered. How did Julian die? I didn't think he would live very long."

"He died of an injury," Karen said. "We don't know if it was accidental or not. We're trying to find out what happened. Do you think Remi might have killed him?"

"Remi loved his babies. I don't know why he would kill Julian."

"Do you have any idea where Remi would have gone?"

Helene seemed calmer. "They said Julian was found in Massachusetts. Remi didn't know anybody down there, but maybe he had an army friend." She thought a moment and continued. "No, Remi didn't have friends. I don't know where he would have gone."

"We believe that they went to a commune in this area. Was Remi into the hippie lifestyle?"

Helene laughed. "Remi was a drunk and a pedophile, but he wasn't a hippie. He was in the army for three years, in Vietnam. But he was bad before he ever went in the army."

Gil asked scooted closer to the camera. "Excuse me, but what did Remi do for a living?"

"Before he got fired, he worked in a sawmill. He ran a buzz saw." Helene seemed emboldened and no longer burdened by upswelling memories. "When you find my daughters, can I talk with them? Visit them?"

Karen gave a hesitant smile. "I'll try to make that happen, Miss Faucher. Thank you for your help."

THIRTY-SEVEN

Dr. Lipton guided Gil's mind back down the escalator and into the movie theater. "Remember, you have the remote and are in control. Any time you want to stop the video, just press pause on your remote. How are you feeling?"

"I feel very relaxed," said Gil.

"Very good. Now go to the last time you dreamed about a snake and press start. Tell me what you see."

Gil pressed a few buttons on the remote. "I'm crawling on the ground as fast as I can. The stones on the ground are sharp, and they hurt my hands and my knees. Blood is dripping from my head. A snake is rearing up, and I headbutt it, then roll away!"

"Press pause. Now take some deep breaths in and out. Each time you breathe, you get more and more relaxed." Craig waited for Gil to breathe. "How do you feel?"

"I feel relaxed."

"Good. Now look around at where the snake was and tell me what you see."

"I see that it wasn't a snake. It was a thick, woody vine. It's hanging from the top of a tall oak tree."

"Good. How do you feel?"

"I feel relaxed."

"Good, now press the play button again and tell me what you see."

Gil says, "I was scared of the vine, so I tried to crawl even faster. I heard a roar and when I look back, a tiger leaped at me!"

"Press pause. Now take some deep breaths in and out. How do you feel?"

"I feel relaxed."

"Good. Now, look back to the tiger and tell me what you see."

"It's not a tiger. It's that little deformed kid. His head is misshapen, and his teeth are misaligned. It looks like he is laughing."

"Good, now press play and tell me what you see."

"I don't see anything. The dream ends."

Craig guided Gil out of his hypnosis. "So what do you think?"

"These nightmares seem to be some kind of hyperexaggeration of things that scared me. They also change each time I have them. Why would I have nightmares? I don't see any benefit to having them."

"There are some theories about the evolutionary benefit of nightmares. The predominant theory is that they may have kept us sensitized to threats we might encounter day-to-day, like dangerous animals or rival tribes. Sometimes the nightmare becomes a stored memory in and of itself, and your mind categorizes the nightmare as a threat, which amplifies it to an absurd level. But these theories are not yet fully confirmed. Animals have nightmares too. Even dogs."

"So maybe I did come in contact with the deformed kid back then."

"Remember, whatever you learned from your hypnosis may put your nightmares into context, but your memories of what actually happened may be far from accurate. Perhaps your anxiety about seeing this child is one source of your nightmares, but there could be more to it. Your head injury could have confused your mind back then."

Gil tried to remember what had happened, but he couldn't.

"By the way," continued Dr. Lipton. "I've been reading up on the hippies. It's so interesting, I really had no idea. It did end up being a kind of peaceful revolution that changed the world in a lot of ways. I still plan to read more about the communes. Living in a commune had to be very different from anything I've experienced."

Inspired by Craig's research, Gil thought he would order some books about the communes in Farnum.

Gil checked into the Hotel Northampton on a Saturday afternoon. After getting settled, he went down to the lobby, where Lili was waiting for him. They were both wearing masks, but they gave each other a friendly hug. They removed their masks after going outside, and Gil said, "I'm concerned that you dressed up so beautifully—I look like a schlub."

"Oh, nonsense! You look very nice. Button-down collars suit you. I thought we could walk around town a little before dinner, and I'll show you my city." As they walked down Main Street, Lili said, "I fell in love with this place when I did my undergrad at Smith College, which is right over that way. I still like the vibe of the college-age crowd. Keeps the city energized."

They crossed the street, put on their masks, and explored Thorne's Marketplace. Inside, three middle-aged women dressed like artsy college kids yelped and gave Lili a hug. One of them asked, "Who's your new friend, Lili?"

Lili made introductions and said, "Gil's from Saratoga Springs. I'm showing him around."

The woman introduced as Veronica laughed and said, "Well, don't do anything I wouldn't do. You might scare him away!"

They parted ways and Gil gave Lili a questioning look.

"Veronica was my most recent love interest. She's a little bit of a wiseass, though."

Gil was taken aback. "Wait, what?"

Lili smiled and shrugged. "I'm very flexible in my ways. Does that bother you?"

Gil raised his eyebrows and said, "No, I don't think so. But I'm not very flexible in my ways. I just like girls, one girl at a time."

"That's fine, Gil. Everyone should just be who they are."

"I think so too, but sometimes it's not that easy to figure out who I am."

THIRTY-EIGHT

Karen checked the caller ID on her office phone, then picked up the line. "Happy Monday, Lili."

"Hi, Karen. We got a hit on the DNA from the rope that was used to hurt Gil. You're not going to believe this, but it's the brother of the deceased child."

"No way! Hold on a minute." Karen looked at her notes and said, "The brother's name was—is—Theo. Any matches in CODIS?"

"Sorry, no. Any connection to the arsons?"

"Not yet. We're still processing evidence from those scenes, but there wasn't much DNA. I'll let you know when I get anything else."

Chief Reyes appeared at Karen's cube. "We got a body."

Karen nodded. "Lili, I got to go. Thanks for calling."

"I'll drive myself and meet you there," said Chief Reyes. "It's on the tracks behind Ryan and Casey's. It looks like it's Sneaky Pete."

Karen grabbed her stuff, went down to her car, and drove the short drive to the railroad tracks behind the package store on Main Street. There were already three cruisers on scene, and the area was taped off. Sergeant Phillips approached her. "Hi, Karen. It's Sneaky Pete. It could be a natural or maybe not. Foamed at the mouth. I called Crime Scene."

"Poor Sneaky. He was a nice guy. He had all those pin-buttons all over his hat and jacket." The sergeant handed her some booties and gloves. She donned them, then she went down the embankment to Sneaky's hovel. Phillips stayed behind to fill in the chief, who'd just arrived.

Sneaky lived in a condominium of a few large cardboard boxes held together with silver duct tape and covered with a blue and a brown tarp. Sneaky was lying on his back, half out of the door flap, his eyes staring lifelessly at the sky. There was dried white foam around his mouth and down his chin and neck. Karen carefully stepped around the area. There was a shopping cart with bags full of clothing and Sneaky's other belongings.

Karen walked back up the hill to talk to the chief. "Well, he OD'd or was poisoned, maybe. If it was murder, it's a different MO than Flannel Man." Flannel Man was a vagrant who was stabbed to death the previous year. They hadn't yet found the murderer. "How long until Crime Scene gets here?"

"Probably a half hour or so," said the sergeant.

Chief Reyes asked, "Do we know Sneaky's real name?" Karen and Sergeant Phillips shook their heads.

"Who found him?" asked Karen.

The sergeant nodded to the left. "Her name's Brenda Sealy. She works at the Mesa Verde restaurant and brings him food most days."

Karen went over to talk to her, but Brenda didn't have much information, so Karen took down her contact information and let her go. "She's got nothing," she told the other officers. "I'll contact Social Services and get Sneaky's info."

"I'll have to make a statement," said Chief Reyes. "Let me know when you have his name and what the Crime Scene guys can tell you. I'm heading back."

Karen walked around the scene some more and took pictures of the few people who were watching. When Crime Scene pulled in, she briefed them on what she knew and exchanged phone numbers. Their leader, Kevin, examined the body for a few minutes. "I'd estimate that he died between 4:00 a.m. and noon. I'll narrow that down later. I can't tell anything from the foaming at the mouth. That could have been caused by a medical problem. Okay if I transport the body?" Karen nodded.

After watching them remove the body, she asked, "Mind if I take a look in the box?"

"As long as you look from outside."

Karen borrowed a flashlight and peered inside. The box looked fairly neat and comfortable. It was carefully lined with blankets and assorted scrap cloth. There was a box of food and bottles of water in one of the annex areas. There was a box of neatly folded clothes and some toiletry supplies. Then she saw a notebook. "Can you process that notebook and transfer it to my custody?" Kevin nodded and asked one of the techs to process the notebook. Karen left with the notebook in hand.

———————

Sneaky's notebook contained extremely detailed notes in tiny but legible handwriting. She focused on the last few pages, which were some sort of thesis on the interconnection of seemingly random things. One section discussed how a group of gray squirrels interacted with each other and acorns from some nearby oak trees. Each of the squirrels had a name. Another section described the connections he observed between various downtown shopkeepers and delivery people. Although strangely compelling, not obviously helpful to her.

Back at the office, she called the nearest Department of Developmental Services rep, who was in Turner's Falls. "Hi, Nancy, this is Detective Karen Tindall with the Greenfield Police Department. Do you know of a homeless guy in Greenfield called Sneaky Pete?"

"Sure, we all know him. His real name is Reginald Hall. What's going on?"

"I'm sorry to say he was found deceased this morning."

"Oh no! He was such a nice man."

"Yes, he was. I'm looking for his next of kin and any other information about him."

"Sure, hold on a second." Karen could hear Nancy rummaging through a file cabinet. "I have his file. He has a brother who lives in Amherst. The easiest thing would be for me to fax you his file. I'll send you the parts that I think you'd want, but if you want to see all the old miscellaneous sheets of counseling sessions and assessments, you can swing by the office. Do you still have a fax machine?"

When the fax machine finished spitting out paper, Karen read the file. She wandered into the chief's office. "Hey, Chief. Sneaky Pete's real name was Reginald Hall. He was only thirty-nine and was working on his PhD in computer science at Tufts when he was diagnosed with schizophrenia. His next of kin is a brother in Amherst. I'm about to call him. Crime Scene says the foaming at the mouth could be the result of natural causes, so we don't know anything yet."

Chief Reyes just grunted.

Karen called Percival Hall and told him about his brother's death. Percival cried. She told him she'd visit him in a couple of days when the autopsy was done.

Karen got a cup of coffee and called Gil. "Hey, Gil. The DNA from the rope that plucked you off your motorcycle is from the brother of the deceased kid."

"No way! Is it Theo?"

"It must be. His name isn't on file anywhere, and his DNA's not in any database. Gil, what's going on? You don't sound too good."

"I got COVID. I feel awful."

"Oh, that's too bad. Are you vaccinated?"

"Yeah, I'm up to date on my boosters, and the doctor gave me some pills, so I should survive."

"Well, take it easy. In the meantime, do you have any idea how we can find Theo?"

"I don't know, my brain isn't as clear as it usually is. Let me think about it and I'll call you back."

———————————

Gil woke up from his third nap of the day. He grimaced as he forced down his pill, hating how it made his whole mouth taste like mercury. But he had to admit he was feeling much better. Just a couple of days before, he'd been feverish and had a bad sore throat. Now it was the eighth day after testing positive, and the only symptoms he had were fatigue and the lack of taste and smell. The fatigue was the worst, but he slept better.

His bowl of chicken-favored ramen didn't taste like anything, but the warmth felt good. When the timer on his cell phone went off, he checked his COVID test. It was negative!

THIRTY-NINE

Chief Reyes woke up to his phone ringing on the nightstand. He answered while his wife grumbled something unintelligible in her sleep.

"Chief, this is Hovis. Karen's missing!"

Reyes bolted up in bed. "What do you mean, missing?"

"Her husband called and said she never came home from work, and her calls go to voicemail. Her car's still here."

"I'll be there in ten. Call in Phillips."

———————

Gil and his pickleball partner were down by two, and the other team was serving for the win. It was a cold September morning, but the players were determined to stay outdoors rather than play in the gym with COVID around. The serve was slow, and Gil returned it with no trouble, then he moved up to play net. On the return, the opposing player hit it softly back up the middle. Gil watched it sail by, as did his partner. Neither had bothered to hit it back. Gil shook his head, and his partner laughed about it. What a way to lose.

When Gil got back to the bench, he checked his phone and found a voicemail from an unknown number with a western Massachusetts area code. He expected it to be the usual solicitation for extending his car's warranty, but instead it was from Chief Reyes asking him to give him a call. Officer Conant answered the phone and put on Chief Reyes. "Gil, we have a big problem. Karen's missing. She didn't return home after work last night. Her husband called it in."

"Oh my God!" Gil felt like he'd been punched in the gut.

"Now I know that the cold case has been on the back burner lately, but that or some of the other cases she's been working on could be related to her disappearance. In particular, there was a DNA hit related to your motorcycle crash that belongs to the brother of the deceased child."

Gil felt exasperated, but he quickly searched his mind for something he could do. "I have an idea about how we can find him, but it's kind of a long shot. I think we should have the local news stations and papers put out Helene Faucher's search for her daughters. Maybe one of the daughters still lives in the area and will contact us to find her mom. Then we can find the brother. I'll be there in about two hours. We've got to find her!"

———————

Gil drove his SUV to the Greenfield Police Station as fast as he could, but he had to park on a side street due to all the pandemonium. He jostled his way past the reporters, and the officer at the door radioed in to get permission for him to enter. In the conference room, officers discussed a list of actions on the big monitor. Everyone was wearing masks. Chief Reyes said, "Everybody, this is Gil Novak from New York. He's been helping Detective Tindall on the cold case. The news interview from Canada was his idea. Gil, this is Franklin County Sheriff Randy DeStefano and Deputy Superintendent Cindy Johnson from the State Police. This is Kenny Tran from the *Greenfield*

Recorder, who's coordinating the news releases. Kenny, please tell us what's going on."

Kenny said, "I've teamed up with the newspaper *Journal Le Nord* and CTV Montreal to write an article and tape an interview on Helene Faucher's search for her long-lost daughters. Their response has been amazing. Both the article and the newscast will be ready late this afternoon. I've arranged for the article to be posted in all the local newspaper electronic and print editions, and the newscast will be picked up by WWLP in Springfield. I'm working to get it on the other stations in the area."

Chief Reyes said, "And these news reports will say nothing about the connection to Karen's disappearance or anything else."

"That's right. This is simply a human-interest story about a woman who was separated from her kids many years ago and is trying to reconnect. We'll talk about the possibility of a commune connection and why we think the daughters could be in this area. I'll need more background on that."

"Okay, Gil," said Chief Reyes. "Please go with Kenny and answer his questions. Avoid all discussion of connections to any possible crimes, including the cold case. This has zero connection to any of our work as far as the public knows. Thanks."

After Gil briefed Kenny Tran on the daughters, he wandered over to Karen's desk to see if there were any clues. He found a folder on her desk labeled "Sneaky Pete." Inside was a fax about Reginald Hall, a.k.a. Sneaky Pete, and a black-and-white picture of Reginald and some of Karen's notes.

Gil felt guilty for nosing around in Karen's file, so he closed the file quickly before anybody walked by.

FORTY

Summer found Luke Forest at the logging area and brought him to Vincent Held's sanctuary. Besides the many Buddhist and Hindu statues, Luke noticed that the room was filled with pictures and paintings of Vincent. It was a shrine to himself, which gave Luke a bad feeling. Summer, Luke, and Vincent sat in comfortable cushioned chairs. Vincent offered Luke some tea, which he politely declined.

"I understand that you'd like to become a member of our community," said Vincent. "Why is that?"

"I feel like I can help out here," said Luke earnestly. "I think I've already helped a lot because I know about logging. Also, I feel like this is a safe place for my family."

Vincent didn't seem convinced. "You're a lot older than most of our members, including me. But as you said, you have a lot to contribute. More than just your experience in logging. You seem to know how to get groups of people to work together to accomplish goals. Most of our people are too young and inexperienced to know how to work together. What do you think about our approach to spiritualism?"

Luke thought for a moment about how honest he should be. "I never really thought much about religion. I only went to church when I was a kid because my mother made me. I'd never done meditation until I came here, and I can't promise I'll take to it, but I'm giving it an honest try. I think it might be good for my family. We've had a rough year, and I think the meditations are . . . calming."

"Very well," said Vincent. "I accept you and your family into our community. I also appoint you leader of our logging crew. Summer, ask Trevor to come and see me. I have something new for him to do."

Summer seemed upset. "Aren't you going to meet with Willow to see what she wants?"

Vincent sighed as if they'd had this type of conversation before. "That won't be necessary. I've accepted Luke and Willow is part of Luke's family. Obviously, Willow will be part of our community."

She formally registered Luke and his family, and she collected all of Luke's remaining cash. As he rejoined the logging crew, she went to find Willow to share Vincent's decision. Summer asked Willow if she wanted to stay and Willow said, "I do want to stay here. I like it here, but . . . never mind."

"Never mind what?"

"It's nothing. We'll see how it goes."

Summer showed Willow her new dorm: a corner area where they could put up some privacy curtains.

"I'd like a bunk bed over here and a single bed there and a crib right there," said Willow. "Then I'd like another privacy curtain between the bunk bed and the single bed."

Summer looked confused by Willow's proposed sleeping arrangements, but she'd talk to the dormitory leader to make the arrangements.

———————

As he always did, Luke sat with Willow and Angel for their rice-and-beans supper to grill them about their days. "Who did you talk to today?"

Willow rolled her eyes. "I talked to April, Annie, Summer, the girls serving lunch and dinner, and some little children. Do you want to know their names?"

"What about guys? What guys did you talk to?"

"While I was in the outhouse, a guy came in, pulled down his pants, and said, 'Excuse me.' I didn't talk to him, and he didn't talk to me."

Luke tried not to show his anger in public. "I told you not to go in there without your sister, or at least another girl! What about Angel? Who did she talk to?" Angel just looked at her plate.

"I'm not with Angel during the day, but you know Angel doesn't talk. She hasn't talked since Jules died."

"But how will I know if a guy starts up with her? Guys won't care if she doesn't talk. Guys might like that she doesn't talk!" Angel's face turned red, and she was shaking. She got up and ran out of the dining hall. Other people around them started to stare.

Luke stood up to go after her, but Willow froze him with her glare. "Leave her alone. She's just going to cry."

The others were staring at him, so he sat back down. He wolfed down his supper and left. Willow cleaned up the table and hurried to their dorm to protect Angel. When she got there, Luke was sitting on Willow's bottom bunk, his arm around Angel, his vile mouth whispering in her ear. Angel was shaking and whimpering.

Willow threw Luke's arm off Angel. "Go! Get out!" she whispered loudly. "You're making it worse." Luke was going to ignore her, but something in her voice made her sound dangerous. He slowly got up, leered at Willow, and walked out.

Over the next few weeks, Luke grew unusually distant from his family, seeing them only when he went to bed. He even avoided Theo. Willow started hanging out with April's circle of friends, which even included a few guys in the commune's band. Their band took the name Starshine. They became bigger, more electric—better—and their singers perfected their three-part harmony. Whenever they played, Willow and Angel would dance, wholly immersed in the music.

One evening at dusk, the band was doing an enthusiastic rendition of "Monday, Monday." The girls were dancing when Angel, her eyes closed as if she was in a trance, started singing in harmony at the top of her lungs. Everyone else stopped dancing, then watched as she kept swaying and spinning and singing to the music. She was singing so loudly that even the band could hear her, and they carefully reduced their volume to give her the spotlight. When the song ended, Angel opened her eyes, suddenly realizing that everyone was staring at her. Her swaying stopped, and Willow put her arm around her to calm her down. The band leader, Gary, left the stage, went over to Angel, and asked if she'd like to join them on stage. Willow expected Angel to panic and run away. But she took Gary's hand and followed him up, joining in a version of "Teach Your Children."

After the concert, Willow picked up Theo and walked toward the stage, eyeing Luke, who stood off to the side. Gary gave Angel a big hug, and Luke swelled with rage. Before Willow could block him, Luke tromped up onto the stage, grabbed Angel by the arm, and tore her away. Willow followed them down a trail to the logging area, but she lost sight of them. She stopped when the trail branched into a whole network of trails. Then she heard Angel screaming. She ran down the hill, choosing a path as the sound echoed off the surrounding hills. She couldn't tell where they were. She frantically went one way, then the other, and finally saw a flash of movement toward the brook. Luke had ripped Angel's clothes off and bloodied her face. He was naked from the waist down and had pinned down her shoulders with his hands. Angel was gasping for breath. Willow put down the baby, grabbed a branch, and swung it at Luke's head. A solid hit.

Luke lay still on the dirt. Willow picked up the baby, grabbed Angel, and ran along the brook. There was a dirty sweatshirt sitting on a log, so she put in on Angel and brought her back to the dorm. Willow had started cleaning Angel's face when a girl she didn't know came into their space. "Hi, Willow," she whispered. "I'm Terry. Could you come here a minute?" They went to the other side of the curtain. "I'm afraid that we need to get you out of here, right now. We'll take you to a safe place. You and your sister need to get your stuff and come with me. This is Carter. He'll help carry your stuff."

After about an hour of driving along dark, winding back roads in Carter's dirty green station wagon, they pulled into the yard of a poorly maintained farmhouse. A girl met them outside and spoke privately and heatedly with Carter. A hatch of flies danced in the headlight beams. Some resolution was found, and the girl came over to Willow. "Hi, my name's Suzanne. We've decided that you should stay here for tonight. Tomorrow we're going to take you to a safer place up in Vermont."

The next morning, Suzanne and a girl called Chickie drove them for another hour to a well-maintained farm. Out front sat a ramshackle farmstand with a multicolored sign that read "Aquarian Agrarians." A girl, Sherry, greeted them and welcomed them to the Peace Out Commune. She gave Chickie and Suzanne hugs and helped bring Willow and Angel's belongings into a recently built cabin filled with bunk beds. They went back outside to a picnic table where another girl brought them some lemonade. "Hi, my name's Tina."

Willow introduced her family. Theo started fussing, so Willow looked around, shrugged, pulled out a boob, and started to breastfeed him. Tina and Suzanne looked at each other and laughed. Willow looked horrified, but Tina quickly said, "Oh no! You're fine—we've just never seen anybody do that before. I think it's amazing!"

A dog ran over to Angel and dropped a stick at her feet. Angel looked at Willow, whose smile assured her. She took the stick and threw it, and the dog chased after it.

"That's Mindy," said Suzanne. "She'd love for you to play with her." When Angel went off to play with the dog, Suzanne looked serious. "Willow, please tell us what's going on."

Willow told them what had happened the day before and felt safe enough to tell them how their father had killed their mother, causing them to flee and end up at Astral Plane.

Suzanne and Tina looked horrified. "Is your father going to come after you?" Tina asked.

"I don't know if he would come after us or try to run from the cops. I worry that the cops will come after us since we probably belong to him, in their eyes."

Suzanne put a hand on her shoulder. "We will you new identities. When that's all settled, where would you like to go?"

FORTY-ONE

Officer Toomey pulled into the parking lot of the Farnum Police Department at exactly 10:00 p.m. He got out of the police car and removed his shotgun from the trunk. He shut the trunk and heard a muffled cry behind him. A hippy guy, bound with rope, was hanging upside down from a rusty climbing peg on a telephone pole. His hair was matted with blood, and he had a cloth gag taped in his mouth.

Toomey pulled the folding knife out of his utility belt and cut the rope, slowly lowering the man. He removed the gag and untied his hands.

"Thank you," said Luke.

"I'm Officer Toomey with the Farnum Police Department. What is your name, sir?"

"I'm Luke, Luke Forest." Luke tried to stand, but he fell back down. "Whoa, dizzy."

"Whoa, sit for a minute. I'm going to call an ambulance."

"No ambulance," said Luke. "No doctors!"

"Okay, okay. Let's go inside and talk." Officer Toomey unlocked the door, and they sat down in an interview room. "Would you like some coffee?"

"Maybe just some water? I'm dying of thirst and gotta pee." Toomey pointed out the restroom.

Luke came back and sat down, chugging the water Toomey gave him. Luke's hands were shaking. "Thanks."

"So, Mr. Forest, how did you come to be hanging from that telephone pole?"

Luke knew he couldn't connect himself with the commune or he'd definitely go to jail. "Some kids did it. I was walking down the road, and they stopped their car and asked me where I was going. I told them I was heading east, and they knocked me down and tied me up. Then they drove me here and hung me on that pole."

"How long were you hanging there? Are you injured?"

"No, I'm okay. I was there for about an hour, maybe more."

"Did you recognize these kids?"

"No, I'm not from around here. I'm from New York."

"Okay, did they steal anything?"

"They took my knapsack which had my wallet in it, but I didn't have much money."

"Can you describe the kids and their car?"

"The car was an old blue Ford—a Fairlane, I think. The boys were about eighteen, had short hair, one blond the rest dark. One had a burn scar on his neck here."

"Okay, Mr. Forest. I just wrote down what you told me. Please read it and sign here." Luke read it and signed. "No reason for us to hold you here. How can I get in contact with you?"

Luke thought about it. "I guess you can't. I'm just kinda passing through. I do want my wallet back, though. Can I just call you in a few days?"

FORTY-TWO

Lili met Gil for dinner at the Hangar Pub and Grill. Both of them looked tired and upset. Lili ordered a burger and a merlot, and Gil ordered a buffalo chicken sandwich and a lemonade. "I'm sorry that this is kind of a miserable date," said Gil.

Lili smiled. "Well, maybe we can keep trying until it's not so miserable."

Gil chuckled. "Why couldn't we just track Karen's cell phone?"

"We did. It was under her car at the station."

The six o'clock local news was wrapping up on the pub's TV. "Tyler, today we have a story out of Canada about a woman named Helene who is looking for her long-lost daughters. This story is being developed by Kenny Tran from the *Greenfield Recorder*. Hi, Kenny. Do we have you?"

Gil asked the bartender to turn it up.

Kenny showed up on video from his computer, a common occurrence during COVID. "Hi, Darcy, I think we're connected."

"So, Kenny, why do you think Helene's daughters may be in this area?"

"Well, Helene's name was originally Jacqui Foy, and she and her daughters originally lived in Keeseville, New York, near the Adirondack Mountains. Back in 1971, Jacqui says her husband, Remi Foy, attacked her, leaving her for dead, and then he took her kids away. Her daughters were named Marie and

Angela Foy. I discovered that the girls and their father ended up living in the communes around here, so they still may be around. As far as the daughters know, their mother died from that attack in 1971."

"Well, that's quite a sad story, Kenny," said Darcy. "She's been searching for her daughters for fifty years? Let's see if our audience can help reunite this family. I'd like to play a tape from Helene for you."

Helene came on the TV and spoke with a French accent. "Hello, my name is Helene. I'm looking for my daughters, Marie and Angela Foy." She held up a picture, and the camera zoomed in on the young girls. "I heard that they may be in your area, and I would desperately like to find them. I tried searching with DNA, but I didn't get any matches yet. Please, if you find my daughters, call Mr. Tran to get in touch with me. Thank you." Kenny showed an old picture of Remi Foy, who was wanted by the New York State Police for questioning in this incident.

———————

The next morning, Gil met Micky Tindall for breakfast at Brad's Place in Greenfield. His old friend looked on the verge of tears and had a streak of anger on his face. "I don't know what I'll do if something's happened to her," said Micky. "I used to worry about her during her first few years as a police officer, but she only had some minor scrapes. She's a tough girl." He was downcast and shaking his head. "Jeff had to be medicated."

"I've been trying to help the police as much as I can," said Gil, "and Chief Reyes has pulled out all the stops. The staties, the sheriff, the crime lab—they're all over it. They'll find her."

"I know I should be back at home with Jane and Jeff, but Jane's beside herself, and Jeff is catatonic. Karen's parents are flying up from Florida, and I have to go pick them up at Bradley Field soon. I needed a break for a few minutes."

"Can you eat some of your breakfast?"

Micky shook his head.

"Well, drink your coffee at least." Gil's phone rang, showing a number from the Greenfield Police Department. "Hello?"

"Gil Novak? This is Officer Weems. Chief wants you back at the station now."

"Okay, I'll be there in five minutes." Gil hung up. "Chief Reyes needs me at the station." Gil left a twenty on the table. "We'll find her!"

———————————

"It worked!" said Chief Reyes. "Kenny got a call from one of the daughters this morning. I sent Sergeant Phillips over with a couple of officers to try and find the son and bring the daughters in for questioning. I'd like you to observe the interviews."

Gil's heart leaped. "Yes, sir!" Reyes led him to a set of chairs to wait. Gil declined coffee. A few minutes later, Lili forced a smile as she and her crew headed out on another assignment. Gil impatiently paced, and after a long while, an officer escorted two nicely dressed women into the interview room. Gil recognized one of them as Pamela, Eddie Locke's girlfriend. He approached the interview room but was miffed when Chief Reyes signaled for him to stay put.

Chief Reyes found Gil sitting a few minutes later. "I basically told them that they had to get a lawyer before I questioned them. It'll probably be an hour or so before we're ready to start, so you could come back later if you want. We'll be interviewing them one at a time."

Gil decided to make a run to Adams Donut Shop while he waited. Along the way, he thought about what the women looked like, but he couldn't connect their faces to the girls he observed so many years before. The fact that Pam was dating Eddie seemed like a bizarre coincidence. He brought back three dozen donuts.

————————

Gil and a few others watched the interview through a one-way mirror.

"I'm Chief Reyes of the Greenfield Police Department. This is an interview of Susan Rasmussen who has not been charged with any crime. This interview is being recorded." He read Susan her rights and asked her lawyer to state his name for the record. "This is Ms. Weeks from Franklin County Social Services who is advising me on this case. Ms. Rasmussen, please state your full name."

"Susan Lee Rasmussen." She sounded a little nervous.

"Is that your legal name?"

She glanced at her lawyer, and he gave her a nod. "I don't think so, no."

"Please state your legal name."

"Marie Elizabeth Foy."

"Please state any other names you've used."

She snickered. "I used the name Willow Forest for a few months when I was a teenager." Her lawyer made a slicing motion to indicate that she should keep her answers short.

"How did you get the name Susan Lee Rasmussen?"

"In the early seventies, I was running away from my father with the help of some friends. When I was brought to the commune at Fipp's Corners in Vermont, a guy there gave me a new identity."

"How old were you then?"

"I was sixteen."

"Why were you running away from your father?"

Susan Rasmussen—Willow—told the chief the whole story, starting with her father's attack on her mother. "I can't believe she's alive! Oh my God!" She burst into tears.

Reyes waited for her to regain her composure. "Would you like some more coffee? Water?"

"More coffee would be nice." Reyes nodded to an officer who went to get some coffee.

After giving her another minute, he continued. "How many children do you have?"

"One."

"What is the child's name?"

"Mark Breen, but that's not his original name either. His birth name was Theo Foy. He was born at home, and his birth was never recorded."

"Who is his father?"

She looked away, embarrassed. "His father was my father." Even though Gil already knew about the incest, he felt himself flush with anger upon hearing it from Susan.

"We're trying to find your son. He is suspected of kidnapping a police officer. Any idea where we should look for him?"

Her lawyer leaned forward. "Let the record show that she has already been asked this question prior to this interview and answered it to the best of her ability and has been fully cooperative with the police. Ms. Rasmussen, you may answer Chief Reyes."

"Mark works for me at Past Times Antique Shop on Routes 5 and 10 in Deerfield. He's our driver and delivers antiques or moves them between the shop and our warehouses. He also fixes things. The warehouses are on Hope Street in Greenfield and on Sherman Drive in Turner's Falls. I've given the addresses to your officers. Mark lives by himself in Greenfield at 15 Larch Street, apartment 2B. I don't know of any other places."

"Does your son own any weapons?"

"He doesn't own any guns or anything, but I'm sure he has kitchen knives and tools. Stuff like that. Mark's a little slow. Please give him a little extra time if you talk to him. When he was a kid, his doctor determined that he was mildly developmentally challenged, and he was in special classes in school. Nowadays, they'd call him 'on the spectrum,' I suppose."

"But he has a driver's license?" asked Chief Reyes.

"He can read and write, and for some reason, he's really good at multiple-choice tests. He can read road signs and maps, but don't expect him to read a book or write an essay. In conversation, he doesn't come across normally. He'll never look you in the eye, and he pauses a while before reacting. But he's never been violent or had any arrests or anything! Please don't hurt him!" Susan put her hand to her mouth to stifle a cry.

"We don't intend to hurt your son, Ms. Rasmussen," Chief Reyes assured. He looked toward the one-way mirror and spoke, "Inform Sergeant Phillips about Mark Breen's condition. Tell him to treat him carefully."

An officer next to Gil pushed a button that activated the intercom in the interview room. "Got it, Chief."

"Gosh, that poor woman," said Gil.

In the interview room, Susan looked more composed, and Chief Reyes continued, "Do you know why he would kidnap a police officer?"

"Don't answer that!" said Susan's lawyer. "It has not been proven that Mr. Breen has kidnapped anybody."

"Okay," said Reyes, taking a breath. "Would Mark have any reason to kidnap a police officer?"

Susan teared up again and answered with a shaky voice. "No, of course not!"

An officer came in with a cup of coffee for Susan and handed Chief Reyes a note from Gil. Reyes read it and asked, "Does Mark know about the cave at Poet's Seat Mountain that you stayed in?"

"Yes, I brought him there a few times when he was a kid."

"When Mark was growing up at the Astral Plane Commune, what buildings did he play in or hide in?"

Susan looked as if the question was absurd, but then a look of possibility came over her. "There were several buildings. Can I draw you a picture?"

Reyes paused the interview for a couple of minute to direct his officers to search the cave and get permission from the land owner to search the commune buildings. He continued, "What happened to your father, Remi Foy?"

"I don't know," she said earnestly. "As I said, when he tried to rape Angela, I hit him in the head with a branch, and he went down and stopped moving. Other people showed up and took us away from the commune. I never heard anything about him again."

"Was he alive when you left?"

Susan thought for a few seconds and looked at her lawyer. He nodded. "I don't know."

"Who were you with just after you hit your father?"

"I don't know. I don't remember. I was in a panic at the time and crying. Also, I didn't know many of the people there. I didn't know the people who took us away."

"How did your son Julian Foy die?"

Susan teared up. "I don't know! As I told you before, my father said it was an accident. I was too afraid to ask him about it again."

"How did you know it was safe to go back to the Astral Plane Commune?"

"I didn't. Not really. The people I was staying with at Fipp's Corners told me my father had left the commune, and they didn't think he'd be coming back. So we went back. It was the best place for us because of their school for Pam, the nursery school for Mark, and the band for Pam's music. We felt safe there because everyone looked after us."

"Did they tell you if he was gone or if he was dead?"

"Don't answer that! Asked and answered."

FORTY-THREE

Karen had decided to limit her yelling to every half hour. It wasn't working anyway, and her throat still stung after vomiting when she awoke from whatever drug was used on her. Her clothes were soiled, since she hadn't had access to a restroom. A dusty wool blanket was keeping her from freezing, and her captor had provided bottles of water with straws sticking out. They were just close enough for her to sip them with feet chained to a sturdy wooden post and her hands locked behind her back with antique-style manacles. The rough-hewn small barn was drafty, and she hadn't heard any sounds except for gusts of wind and some crows.

She hadn't seen her captor yet, and she assumed she was into her second day of being held against her will. The strangest thing was that she still had her gun in her holster. Who would do that? She knew it was the brother of the deceased child, but who was he? Suddenly, she thought that she was hearing the very distant sound of a siren on the wind. Yes, she was definitely hearing it. Heavy footsteps come up behind her. As she twisted around to see, a burlap bag swallowed her head. She yelled and bucked violently as her captor sprayed something noxious into her. Karen's world went black.

Chief Reyes was questioning Angela Foy, who was now known as Pamela Leone. She had a different lawyer than her sister. One of the officers told Gil that she was somewhat of an area celebrity, being the lead singer of a long-standing rock band called Soundslip. She also owned the art gallery in the same building as Susan's antique shop.

"Do you have any children?" Chief Reyes asked.

"No."

"What is your relationship to Mark Breen?"

Pam chuckled. "I don't know what he is to me, scientifically speaking, but I consider him to be my nephew. He's my sister's son, but my father was his father. He's also my employee. He helps me with my gallery and is a roadie for my band."

An officer came into the interview room and handed Reyes a note. Reyes suspended the interview and excused himself. He left the room and called Sergeant Phillips, who said, "Karen was here in Farnum at what used to be part of the commune. She was kept in a small barn, but she's gone. Her pants and underpants are here, soiled. There are bottles of drinking water, so it looks like Breen is keeping her alive. No sign of her gun. Crime Scene is on their way. Where to next?"

"I'm interviewing the other sister now," said Reyes. "I'll see if I can find more places to search."

Gil had overheard the conversation. "Did you search the places that had arsons?"

Reyes said to Phillips, "Search the places where Karen was investigating arsons." He hung up and told an officer to work on that. Then, back in the interview room, he said, "Mark Breen is suspected of kidnapping a police officer, and we're searching for him. Do you know of any places that he would hide if the police were searching for him?"

Her lawyer held up his hand to stop Pam from answering. "Let the record show that Ms. Leone has answered this question when first contacted by the police." He looked at Pam and said, "You may answer the question."

"Other than his apartment and our warehouses, I don't know of any more places to look."

"Where are the warehouses located?" Reyes asked.

"There's one on Sherman Drive in Turner's and one on Hope Street in Greenfield." She thought for a few seconds. "Before we got the one on Sherman Drive, we had a smaller warehouse on Pierce Street in Greenfield." She gave Reyes directions, and he gave the order through the one-way glass.

They discussed the history of what happened to Pam and her family from the beginning, and the story matched what Susan had described. Reyes asked if she stayed in contact with any of the commune members. She provided a few names, the same ones Susan provided.

FORTY-FOUR

July 1972—Astral Plane Commune, Farnum, Massachusetts

Marie was no longer Willow; she was Sue. Angela was now Pam, and Theo was Mark. After they received their new identities, they stayed at the Peace Out Commune in Vermont for a couple of months before returning to Astral Plane. Susan felt they were safe there, especially after how they'd looked out for her.

Sue was watching Mark play with the other toddlers when she made an upsetting realization. He wasn't toddling. By sixteen months old, the other babies were walking, but Mark wasn't even pulling himself up to stand. He wasn't babbling either. Knowing something wasn't quite right with him broke her heart, but she wasn't surprised. This was another result of her father's evil. Theo needed to see a doctor.

Sue explained her concerns to the nurse in the emergency room at Athol Memorial Hospital. The nurse looked at her compassionately and asked, "Do you have health insurance or money to pay a doctor?" She didn't, so the nurse wrote her a note. "This isn't really an emergency department issue. Go across the street and give this to Caroline at the front desk. She'll get you in to see Dr. McCann, and they won't charge you." She smiled and added, "I hope everything turns out okay for you, dear."

Dr. McCann was in his early forties. He wore big, thick glasses, and his hair was slicked back with Brylcreem. He gave Mark an overall exam and spent some time checking his reflexes and reactions to moving light and sounds. "I'm afraid that Mark is showing signs of mental retardation," he said. "I'm so sorry." Willow started to sob. The doctor handed her a tissue and gave her a minute. "His head is a little small for his age and overall size. Did he have any health issues at birth?"

Willow debated whether she should spill the beans. She couldn't think of any reason to hold back, so she said, "Mark was born from incest. My father started raping me when I was twelve. My first baby was very deformed. He died last year when he was two."

The doctor tried his best to not look as shocked as he was. "Is your father still raping you?"

"No, last year I hit him over the head with a branch when he tried to rape my little sister. He's gone now."

Doctor McCann didn't know if she meant her father was dead or just gone away, but he decided not to pursue that line of questioning. What did the doctors say about your first child?"

"He never went to a doctor. He was born at home. So was Mark."

"Well, we're going to help you with your baby, Sue. Time will tell how mild or severe your son's deficits will be. But getting him started with therapy for his developmental needs will help him be the best that he can be. The state will pay for his needs. I'll have Caroline set you up. You can bring Mark here for his medical care, and I won't charge you. How old is your sister?"

"Pam's thirteen."

"She's still young enough to see a pediatrician. Why don't you make an appointment with Caroline, and I'll give her a checkup too? I'll also see if we can find you a general practitioner who'll see you for free."

————————————

When Sue got back to the nursery school, she told Natalie, her assistant, what the doctor had said. Sue started to sob again. Natalie took Mark and put him down with the other kids, then gave Sue a long hug. "I'm so sorry, Suzie. Let's see what the specialists say, and we'll help Mark as much as we can." Sue was calming down, so Natalie felt she could relay a message. "By the way, Noreen asked to see you while you were out. She said it wasn't urgent."

Willow's chest tightened with worry. She'd been waiting to hear back from Noreen. She ran down the stairs to Pam's classroom and knocked softly at the entryway since there was no door. Noreen looked over. "Well, class, we have a special visitor. Come on in, Sue."

The students all stood and started singing the chorus to "Aquarius/Let the Sun Shine In."

When they finished, Noreen announced, "Today I have the honor to present Susan with a certificate for completing all the requirements of her General Educational Development program. That's the same as graduating from high school! She received very high scores on her test. Let's give her a hand, and then we'll have cake!"

Noreen had organized the other teachers to help Sue and a few other commune members prepare for their GED tests. She gave her a little hug, then Pam gave her sister a bigger one.

————————————

Pam set Mark in an old highchair next to the dining table. Sue brought over a tray with dinners and water to drink. Rice and beans, as usual, but there was also summer squash with onions—a welcome change. It was July, and the early vegetables were being harvested. The farming efforts in the commune had turned out to be quite successful.

As they ate, Sue told Pam about Mark's doctor visit. Pam, of course, knew the risks with babies born of incest. Sue also told Pam that she would have a physical exam in a couple of weeks. Pam just kept eating and didn't say anything.

FORTY-FIVE

August 1973—Astral Plane Commune, Farnum, Massachusetts

It was twilight. Vincent Held had given his sermon, which had sounded more like a corporate presentation about growth and profits than spirituality and supporting each other. The commune band, Starshine, was charging through its playlist for the night, with the vocalists singing masterful harmonies in their version of "Carry On." Pam was their shining star in a blue tie-dyed T-shirt, white overalls, and no shoes. Now tall for thirteen years old, she was starting to look like a young lady.

The field was full. The commune had more than doubled its size, and so had the number of amps. Everyone could hear them, and they even had a sound engineer set up in the back of the audience to make sure the sounds were properly balanced. At the end of the songm there was lots of hooting and whistling and enthusiastic applause. Then the band played "In the Year 2525" for the first time, which unfortunately had more of a tone of despair than hope.

Mark was two and a half and was finally toddling around the blanket. Susan was sandwiched between two guys vying for her attention, but who were apparently willing to share. The smell of sandalwood incense filled the air, which was good because the two guys didn't smell very good. The band transitioned to "Ain't No Sunshine," and Susan grabbed up Mark and started to dance to the slow, deep rhythm. The two friendly guys popped up to dance, then the people adjacent to them. Within a minute, the whole crowd was up swaying and spinning. The crowd joined in to sing the chorus, which the band extended for everyone's enjoyment. It was one of those magical moments that kept the commune going and growing.

———————————

The next day, Susan left Mark with one of the other girls so she could take the ever-taller Pam to get clothes at Rockdale's in Turner's Falls. Susan found Pam squaring off against an older teenage boy who was trying to calm her down. "Hey, I was just trying to be friendly!" said the bow. "You don't have to freak out!"

Susan got between them. "I don't think she wants to be friends, so you should go." The boy dropped his head in disappointment and quickly walked away. Susan gathered Pam in her arms. "It's okay, it's okay. He just likes you."

Pam was sobbing. "I can't, I can't! Maybe never."

"Maybe someday you will want a boyfriend, but it's also okay if you don't. But whatever happens, you're going to need to steer boys away calmly instead of confronting them. Someday you'll need to find a way to make some friends your age. We'll get some help with this. Let's start by getting you some new clothes, okay?"

FORTY-SIX

September 2021—Montague, Massachusetts

Karen came to with a splitting headache. She bent toward a bottle of water to drink, noticing she was in a new place: an old brick building full of dated furniture. It was one of her warehouses. There wasn't much light. Under her blanket, she wore nothing but her socks from the waist down. She didn't feel as though she'd been raped, but it scared her. This building wasn't as cold as the last one, but it wasn't warm either. Her leg shackles bound her to a metal post that ran from floor to ceiling. She tried pulling away to see if it was loose, but it was solid. Her gun lay out of reach in its holster on a box on the other side of the post.

She sipped the water. Next to it was a bottled chocolate nutritional drink, also with a straw in it. It tasted wonderful. She heard a creak to her left and, out of the corner of her eye, saw a young boy's head duck down beyond a darkly stained bureau. "Hello over there!" Her throat was still hoarse, but she tried to sound as calm as possible. "My name's Karen. Please come and talk with me."

The small head slowly rose from behind the bureau, and it turned out to be sitting on the large body of a strong but slightly obese man. He slowly walked over to Karen, his eyes trained on her. His close-cropped dark hair was starting to gray, so he was probably in his late forties or early fifties. If he was the brother of the deceased child, that tracked. He was tall—over six feet tall—and wore black slacks and a dark-brown mid-length jacket over a navy-blue pocket T-shirt. He didn't say anything.

"My name's Karen, and I'm a police officer, but I think you know that. What's your name?" He didn't answer. She felt as though he had a mental deficit of some sort.

"Thank you for the water and the chocolate drink. Why are you keeping me here? My family needs me back home."

"I don't want you to take my mom away," he said, his voice unexpectedly high and childlike.

"What's your name?"

"Mark."

"Mark, why would I take your mom away?"

"Bad things happened a long time ago. We changed our names so nobody could find us."

"Do you know what happened a long time ago?"

"No."

"Well, it's my job to find out what happened. I won't hurt your mom. I know you care for your mom, and you want to protect her, but my kids care for their mom, too, and they're very worried about me. Could you let me go home to my kids?"

Mark thought for a long minute, then approached Karen. Panic took her, then she felt two large keys fall into her lap. Mark quickly left the building.

Karen struggled to fit the key into the antique manacles to release her hands from behind her back, but adrenaline prevailed. Once free, she rubbed her ankles and wrists and stood up. She felt dizzy for a moment, and then her blanket fell. She'd forgotten she was naked from the waist down. She grabbed her holster, but left the gun snapped in. She found the door that Mark used to leave, next to which she found the light switch. The room filled with bright yellow light, and she looked around to find some pants. Among the antiques throughout the building, all she found to wear was a rack of antique dresses.

That evening, a cruiser from the Montague Police Department pulled up to the Greenfield Police Station, and an officer opened the back door so Karen could get out. Jeff ran over to his wife and was about to give her a hug, but instead he pulled up short and took a look at her outfit. Under her uniform jacket, she had an elegant, pink, floor-length chiffon dress with her holster and gun at the waist. Jeff laughed and gave her a big hug. "You really don't smell very good."

Chief Reyes asked, "Are you hurt?"

"No, but I was drugged a couple of times. I'm feeling a little shaky."

"Okay, you're going to the ER to get checked out. I'll drive."

"After I shower and change first. Jeff, please go get me some clothes."

FORTY-SEVEN

Karen had checked out of the ER and was home for the first time in three days. She and Jeff bought a pizza, and she reunited with her kids, who had been looked after by Jeff's mother throughout the ordeal. Lots of hugs, lots of tears. A police officer was guarding their house.

Karen already felt much better in the morning and, despite her husband's protests, went right back to work. She met with Chief Reyes, Sergeant Phillips, Lili D'Amico, and Gil Novak to provide a debrief. "I don't think Mark Breen is much of a danger to anyone, but we definitely need to bring him in."

"I want to bring him in before I let Kenny Tran print the kidnapping story," said Reyes. "That said, he's already figured out a lot. Thoughts on where to look for Breen? We searched his apartment, found his van, and disabled the truck he drives for work."

Gil said, "So far, he's stuck to places he's familiar with, and I think the number of places like that is limited. We should look at those places again and find out if he's lived or worked anywhere else."

"Besides that," said Reyes, "we still don't know what happened to Remi Foy or how Mark's brother died. Remi's name and his alias don't get hits in any online searches or public databases."

"What's happening with Susan Rasmussen and Pam Leone?" asked Karen.

"ADA Chen says that they aren't going to charge them with identity theft since they were minors at the time. The Federal

District Court will decide what happens with their identities. We still need to arrange for Susan and Pamela to meet their mother. I'd like to have Mark Breen in custody before that happens."

"I got the impression that Helene was disgusted by the existence of her grandchildren," said Gil. "We need to be careful there."

"I'm not sure Crime Scene will be of much help," said Lili. "We're almost done processing the warehouse, but I don't think we'll find anything that will help us find Mark Breen."

Reyes nodded. "Okay, I'll talk to Kenny Tran to see if we can put out Mark's picture and arrange for Helene Faucher to reunite with her daughters. Karen, you and Gil go talk to the commune people and see if we can find out what happened to Remi Foy. Phillips, you find Mark Breen."

Karen said, "Since Mark's main concern is protecting his mother, I think he'll keep an eye on her. We should watch her home and business."

When Karen walked with Gil back to her desk, she found a picture stuck to her shelf that read, "Welcome Back Princess!" In the picture, she wore a pink dress and holster, but someone had edited in a tiara and a magic wand. Gil chuckled. Karen rolled her eyes as snickers circulated around the office.

While Karen talked to Sergeant Phillips about staking out Susan Rasmussen, Gil called Terry Billings and got contact information for a few more folks from the commune. Karen said to Gil, "We need to go talk to them in person. If they were involved, they'll probably lie to us, so we need to look them in the eye."

Two of the contacts were in the area, and although both of them said they'd heard about the incident, neither had witnessed it or knew who Remi was. They provided a few more names, but everyone had the same answer.

At the station, Karen asked, "Did anybody seem like they were lying?"

"Not that I could tell, but that's not my area of expertise," said Gil.

"I think they were telling the truth. I guess we'll just have to find more commune members and interview them."

"We have some more names," Gil said, "but they aren't in the area."

Lili rushed over to Karen's desk. "You are not going to believe this. Susan Rasmussen and Pamela Leone have a half brother in Maine!"

Karen gasped. "What?"

"My forensic genealogist found a match on one of the commercial DNA search databases. It's a son of Remi Foy."

"Oh my God!" said Karen. "He wasn't killed at the commune."

"Here's his phone and address. His name is Aaron Foy. He doesn't have a record. I couldn't find any contact info for Remi Foy."

"Cornish, Maine?" Karen googled it and parsed the results. "It's in the middle of nowhere. It's a three-and-a-half-hour drive. I can't go right now."

"I'll go," said Gil.

"No way," said Karen. "You almost got killed last time."

Lili smiled. "I can go with him. I'll coordinate with the Maine staties." Karen gave Lili the hairy eyeball.

FORTY-EIGHT

They met in a conference room at a small Maine State Police outpost in Alfred. State Police Detective Miles brought in Aaron Foy—a burly guy with thinning brown hair and a big bushy beard. Everybody sat at a distance from each other, and the window was open for ventilation so they could drink coffee and eat donuts maskless. The room was pretty cold.

"Hello, Mr. Foy. I'm Lili D'Amico from the Massachusetts State Crime Lab, and this is our consultant, Gil Novak. We're investigating a set of related incidents dating back to 1971, and some of them involve your father, Remi Foy, and his children."

Aaron rolled his eyes. "My father's name was Doug, not Remi. I don't know any Remi Foy."

Lili was writing on her pad. "DNA analysis shows that your father was a man named Remi Foy. He had a warrant out for his arrest in New York State, so he likely changed his name. He was also known as Luke Forest at one point. What was his full name, please?"

"My father's name was Douglas R. Foy. I don't remember what the 'R' stood for. Wait, should I have a lawyer?" asked Aaron.

Lili said, "You can have a lawyer present if you want, but none of these incidents involve you."

"Good. But I don't want to say anything that will get my brother or sister in trouble."

Lili raised her eyebrows. "Oh, none of this would involve those family members either, Mr. Foy. These things happened before any of you were born. Is your father still alive?"

""Nah, he died of liver failure about twenty-five years ago. He was a drunk." He hesitated a moment. "Slow down a minute. You just said this involves my father and his children."

Lili smiled. "Your father had other children, Mr. Foy. You have two half sisters."

He blinked several times and took a deep breath. "Whoa. That's . . . wow. Okay then. What incidents are you talking about? And please just call me Aaron."

"I'll get into that shortly."

"Is your mother still alive?"

"Yeah, she lives in South Portland."

"Please tell me the names of your mother and your siblings."

"My mom is Regina Levine. My brother is Chris Foy, and my sister is Carly Pelletier." He looked up their phone numbers and addresses on his cell phone and wrote them down for Lili.

"What do you do for a living, Mr. Foy?"

"I'm a carpenter, a cabinet maker. What's this all about, anyway? I've answered your questions."

"Fair enough. Gil, why don't you take him through the high points."

"Okay, but this is going to be kind of a disturbing story," said Gil. "In 1971, your father was living with his first wife and two daughters in northern New York State. He'd abused his older daughter and had two sons by her."

Aaron had a disgusted look of disbelief on his face.

Gil continued. "He attacked his wife and left her for dead. He took off with his children and grandchildren, and they ended up camping in a cave in Greenfield, Massachusetts. The older child was about two years old and severely deformed.

191

That child died under suspicious circumstances and was buried in the cave. The family left their cave and went to live in a nearby hippie commune. At some point, your father tried to abuse his younger daughter, and the older one hit him in the head with a stick, apparently knocking him out. Some of the commune members helped the girls escape and change their identities. The girls didn't know if your father was dead or alive."

"It turns out that their mother didn't die after all. For fifty years, they thought she was dead. They're waiting to meet her again, too, but she lives in Canada. Things are a little complicated with COVID."

Aaron was trying to calm himself by breathing slowly and deliberately. "Jeez, I don't even know what to say about any of that. My dad did that?"

"He did," said Lili. "Now that you know the story, are you satisfied that you can continue without an attorney present?"

He thought for a few seconds. "Sure, there's no way this can come back on me. I wasn't even born yet! When I was really young, my father was a normal dad. He went to work and watched my football games. But then he started drinking and beating up my mother. When I was seven, my mother left him, and we moved us to Portland. I never saw him again. After a few years, my mother married Jerry Levine. Great guy. At some point, Mom told us our father had died."

"We'd like to talk to your mother," said Lili.

"Sure, I think she'd appreciate knowing about this. It might explain some of my father's demons. I'll let her know we're coming, and you can follow me there. Hey, can we meet my half sisters?"

Gil smiled. "I'll ask them, but this was all very traumatic for them. Don't get your hopes up."

———————————

The Levine house sat just a block away from the harbor in South Portland. Aaron brought Lili and Gil inside, where they met Jerry and Regina Levine. They looked to be in their mid-seventies, but at first glance, Regina could have been mistaken for a fourteen-year-old girl. She was very petite, with straight blonde hair and a heart-shaped, welcoming face. Gil and Lili looked at each other knowingly. Remi was nothing if not consistent.

Regina sat on the couch between Jerry and Aaron, while Lili and Gil sat in comfy chairs. As Gil went through the story, each recounted event visibly caused Regina pain. By the end, she looked frail and had teared up. Aaron brought her a glass of water, and she took some sips. "When I first met Dougie," she said, "he was the answer to my dreams! He was very handsome, a foreman at a lumber mill, and he had a lot of friends. For a few years, he was great with our kids, and we were very happy. At some point, cracks started to appear in his personality, and his decline was very fast. After hitting me a few times and threatening the kids, I got out of there as fast as I could. I felt lucky that he didn't come after us, but I always worried he would. He was a monster with dark secrets and just couldn't keep it together. I never knew he had a predilection for young girls, but I know I . . . Jesus!" She burst into sobs.

Gil passed over a tissue. "Did Dougie tell you anything about his previous family?"

193

Regina stifled more sobs. "He told me he was married when he was young, but that his wife died suddenly due to bleeding in her brain."

"Not a total lie," said Gil. "Or so he thought. She's actually still alive. Technically, your marriage to him wasn't ever valid." Regina's jaw dropped, but Aaron burst out laughing.

Aaron said, "Living in sin, as you used to say! The coolest thing is that I have more sisters!"

Regina smiled. "That's you, Aaron. Always looking on the bright side."

———————————

Gil looked online and found a bed and breakfast overlooking nearby Casco Bay. He showed the details to Lili on his phone.

"One room or two?" she asked.

Gil's eyes lit up.

FORTY-NINE

By the time Lili and Gil got back to the Greenfield Police Station, Mark Breen had been taken into custody by the State Police in Northampton. He'd been found up in a tree watching his mother's house. Chief Reyes convened a meeting with ADA Chen, Detective Tindall, State Police Detective Devane, Sergeant Phillips, Agent D'Amico, and Gil Novak. Karen showed a slideshow on the monitor to summarize the investigation. Lili's phone buzzed, and she left the room.

"So as far as prosecutions go," said Karen, "we have Mark Breen on attempted murder and kidnapping, but the arsons are still waiting to be confirmed. The courts will have to work out what to do with the family's false identities. The many crimes committed by Remi Foy went with him to his grave. There isn't any proof of a crime that caused the death of Julian Foy. That's it."

ADA Chen said, "Mark Breen will be prosecuted, but because he is mentally challenged, his sentencing will probably be some kind of supervised release program since he's not inherently violent. We should go overboard and make sure he meets with competent counsel and is represented at any interrogations."

"Excuse me," said Gil. "Something still doesn't add up here. Mark Breen is an inherently nonviolent person with low intelligence. I'm amazed that he even has a driver's license. How did he know when I would be on my motorcycle headed to New Hampshire, and how did he come up with the idea to rig a rope across Route 2? How did he know how to drug Karen and kidnap her, much less move her while avoiding detection? And if he's involved in the arsons, how did he know to dodge the cameras? I think someone else is pulling his strings."

Lili came back into the room, and all eyes turned to her. "Well, I've got some interesting news. First of all, we have Mark Breen's DNA from two of the arson scenes, and he had a burn that was professionally treated on his right arm. On the other hand, we also have DNA from a pair of work gloves from an unidentified female at the Montague warehouse scene. There aren't any women involved with their operation, according to the owner. The DNA didn't have a match in CODIS, so we're having it checked by our forensic genealogist."

Chief Reyes said, "Well, that confirms him at the arsons, but Gil makes a good point. It looks like we definitely have more work to do. By the way, Kenny Tran has arranged for Helene Faucher to reunite with her daughters the day after tomorrow. I'm going to put him in touch with Detective Tindall and Gil Novak to get the whole story."

FIFTY

Karen's phone rang while she and Jeff were watching an episode of *Death in Paradise*. She liked the idea of solving absurd murders in a tropical paradise.

Over the phone, Sergeant Phillips said, "We have an arson at a maintenance shed at the fairgrounds. There was a woman in there, and she's on her way to the hospital. She's got burns and smoke inhalation and the EMTs aren't sure how serious it is."

"Do you know who she is?"

"No ID yet."

The officer at the gate let Karen drive into the fairgrounds, and she drove over to the flashing lights. She shivered when she got out of the car, and she could see her breath. The air smelled putrid, like burning rubber. The shed that burned was bigger than she'd imagined, maybe twenty by thirty feet. It was painted white, but about a third of it was charred.

"Same as the others," Sergeant Phillips said. "Gasoline poured through a broken window. The gas can is intact. Crime Scene guys will be here in a few minutes. Still no ID on the woman."

"What's in the shed?"

"A lot of tools, hoses, fan belts—stuff like that."

"Who reported it?"

"There were 911 calls from two neighbors."

"Well, give me their info, and I'll go talk to them. Are there any security cameras?"

"There are. I asked the DPW guys to get me the files."

Karen got the caller info and drove over to the aptly named Fairview Street. About a dozen people were standing together watching the fire department. Karen took their picture with her phone, held up her badge, and said, "My name is Detective Tindall. I'm looking for Richie Peretti and Alma Suarez." Richie and Alma approached Karen and introduced themselves. "I'd like to speak to you separately, please. I'll start with Ms. Suarez." They walked about twenty feet away, and Karen said, "Ms. Suarez, please tell me what you saw before you called 911."

"Please call me Alma." She spoke with a very slight Hispanic accent. "My husband Martin and I were watching TV, and during a commercial, I went into the kitchen to get a drink of water. When I walked through the dining room, I saw the fire. I called Martin to come and look, and he said it looks like a building's on fire. That's when I called 911."

"Did you or your husband see anybody near the fire or at the fairgrounds?"

"No, not until the fire department showed up."

"Is there anything else you noticed? Did you see anybody there during the day?"

"No, that's all I saw."

"Okay, thank you for calling 911. You may have helped save someone's life."

Alma's breath caught, and she put her hand over her mouth.

"Alma, here's my card if you think of anything else that could help me. Please send Richie over."

Richie hadn't seen anyone. All he saw was the fire.

Karen went back to the crowd. "There was a woman in the shed, and she was injured. She's been taken to the hospital. Does anyone know who she might be?" Nobody answered. "Did anybody see anybody at the fairgrounds today or anytime recently?" Nobody answered. "Okay, thanks. Please talk to your kids. They may have seen somebody or something. If you think of anything else, please call me at the police station. Alma and Richie have my cards."

Karen went back to the fairgrounds, where Chief Reyes was talking to Sergeant Phillips.

"Hey, Chief. I talked to the neighbors who are standing over there watching. None of them saw anybody. I'll go to the hospital and see if I can talk to the victim. By the way, I saw Scarecrow skulking over there." Scarecrow was Paula Metz, a reporter from the *Greenfield Recorder*. The origin of her nickname was obvious to anyone who looked at her. Chief Reyes grumbled.

"Hank Wills from the DPW is emailing us the security camera files," said Sergeant Phillips. "I'll meet you back at the station."

Karen said, "Well, we know it wasn't set by Mark Breen. He's in jail."

FIFTY-ONE

Karen entered the emergency room entrance of Baystate Franklin Medical Center. Officer Weems was drinking coffee from a mug while guarding the double doors leading to the treatment area. "Anything?" Karen asked.

"Nothing yet," said Weems. "Scarecrow showed up, and I told her no comment and suggested that she wouldn't get any information here tonight."

"I'll see if I can talk to the doc." Karen went to the guy at the front desk, showed her badge, and said, "Hi, I'm Detective Tindall. I'd like to talk to somebody about our fire victim."

The man at the front desk was a small, skinny guy named Robert, and he looked like he knew what he was doing. "I'll call back and get someone. Would you like some coffee?"

"Sure, that'd be great! Cream and no sugar, please."

Robert made a call on his headset, then brought Karen an ugly green mug that read "Green Wave"—the high school's sports team. The coffee was good, though. After a few minutes, a doctor came out looking for a detective. Karen waved, showed her badge, and introduced herself.

"I'm Doctor Kappas. Do you have any information on our fire victim?"

"Nothing yet. We're looking through the scene to try and find an ID."

"She's very dirty. Might be homeless."

"Will she survive? Can I talk to her?"

"She has some bad burns on her skin and respiratory tract damage due to smoke inhalation. We've sedated her. I'd say she eventually will be okay, even with those burns, but that would be my assessment of a normal, healthy person. I'd need to know her medical history. I don't know yet when you'll be able to talk to her."

"Okay, here's my card. Please give me a call, day or night, when I can talk to her. Someone is out there trying to kill people. I'll be by in the morning to hopefully give you guys more information, but I need to take her picture now so we can talk to Developmental Services and see if they can ID her." Doctor Kappas led Karen back to the fire victim so she could take her picture.

Karen went back to the office and looked at her email, but there weren't any security videos from the DPW yet. She called Chief Reyes, gave him an update on the fire victim, and told him she'd be back in the morning.

FIFTY-TWO

Gil was in his hotel room, reading a novel on his Kindle. It was after midnight, and he was yawning quite a bit, so he decided to go to sleep. While he started to undress, there was a light knock at the door. He looked through the peephole and saw a fidgeting crime scene agent. He let Lili in.

"I need to crash," Lili said, "but I'm all wound up." She started to tear up, and her voice started to break. "I've been going full tilt for days, and, um, I guess I could use a friend."

Gil embraced Lili and felt her shaking ease. He asked, "Would you like something to drink? I have tap water and caffeinated coffee."

Lili chuckled. "Just keep holding me, please."

After a couple of more minutes, Gil said, "Why don't we get in bed, and you can tell me about your day."

They both sat in bed wearing their underwear. Lili talked about what kind of cases her team was working on, interspersed with discussions about personality conflicts, power struggles, and office drama. Gil listened, occasionally restating what she was saying to him, the way Dr. Lipton did. Active listening, Gil knew.

After a while, Gil could tell that Lili was losing steam. "I think you're getting tired, so I'm just going to shut off the light." They lay down, and within a minute, Gil could hear Lili's breathing take on a constant rhythm. He fell asleep a few minutes later.

———————————

Gil woke up at six thirty, thrilled that he had slept like a log. He was doubly thrilled that Lili was still there. They got ready for the day and grabbed a light breakfast in the hotel lobby.

"What are your plans today?" Lili asked.

"I have to sit in on Mark Breen's interrogation at one."

Lili said, "I could take this morning off. Would you like to go on a bike ride this morning? I know a good place. We can rent you a bike."

They went to the Norwottuck Rail Trail near Amherst. Gil was thrilled. The trail had forests and fields, brooks and ponds, and the highlight was a long bridge over the Connecticut River. They stopped at the bridge to take in the scenery, and they saw herons, geese, ducks, and a kingfisher. After returning Gil's rental bike, they ate lunch at the Hangar Pub before parting ways.

FIFTY-THREE

Gil was sitting with Karen at the State Police barracks in Northampton. They were in the observation room adjacent to the interview room where Mark Breen was being interrogated by Detective Devane. Karen whispered to Gil, "That lawyer has a nice suit. He's probably not a public defender." Karen wasn't permitted to be in the interrogation room because she was the kidnap victim.

Detective Devane started the video recorder, stated who was present, and read Mark his rights. "Mr. Breen, you are being questioned because we think you hurt Mr. Gil Novak while he was riding his motorcycle. We think you set some fires, and we think you kidnapped Detective Karen Tindall of the Greenfield Police Department. Did you do these things?"

Mark looked at his lawyer who nodded to him. Mark said, "Yes."

"May I call you Mark?"

His lawyer nodded to him, and he said, "Yes."

"Thank you, Mark. Why did you hurt Mr. Novak?"

Mark looked at his lawyer who again nodded. "Gil Novak is helping the police put my mom and auntie in jail."

"Why would your mom and auntie go to jail?"

"They found Julian's skeleton."

"Why would your mom and auntie go to jail because they found Julian's skeleton?"

Mark looked flustered. He looked at his lawyer, who shook his head. "I don't know," said Mark.

"Did someone tell you that they would go to jail?"

Mark looked distraught and yelled out, "I don't know!"

Detective Devane let Mark calm down for a little while and asked, "Mark, would you like something to drink?"

Mark looked at his lawyer, who nodded his head. "Mountain Dew." He pronounced *mountain* with a strong *t*. The lawyer requested water, so Devane suspended the interview and got drinks.

Once Mark had a chance to gulp down some soda, Detective Devane restarted the interview. "Mark, where did you get the rope that hurt Mr. Novak."

"From Mo."

Gil looked at Karen, who looked at Gil and shrugged.

"What is Mo's last name?" Devane asked.

Mark shrugged.

Please answer in words for the recording."

Mark said, "I don't know. His name is Mo."

"Is Mo your friend?"

Mark looked flustered again. "I don't know."

"Did Mo tell you how to put up the rope to hurt Mr. Novak?"

"Yes."

"Is Mo and man or a woman?"

Mark croaked out something like a laugh and said, "Mo is a man."

"How did you know where and when to put up the rope?"

"Mo told me."

"What was going to happen to Mr. Novak when you put up the rope?"

Mark looked at this lawyer who nodded. "Mr. Novak would get hurt real bad."

Detective Devane looked up at the one-way mirror, ad Karen texted Phillips to work with the staties to find Mo.

"Why did you set the fires?" Devane asked.

Mark looked flustered. "It would keep the police busy, and they wouldn't have time to take Mom and Auntie to jail."

"Who told you that?"

"Mo."

"Where did you get the cans of gas?"

"They weren't cans. Cans are metal."

"Where did you get the containers of gas?"

"Some from the shed and some from Mo." Mark downed more Mountain Dew.

"What does Mo look like?"

Mark looked confused, then looked to his lawyer. The lawyer nodded. "He wears black jeans and a blue hoodie."

"Is he tall?"

"He's shorter than me."

"Does he have white skin?"

"No, he has skin-colored skin, like mine."

"Does he have long yellow hair?"

He chuckled. "No, he has brown curly hair!"

"Does he talk like you?"

"No, he has a lower voice."

"Where does he work? In an office?"

"No, he drives a truck like me."

"Why did you kidnap Detective Tindall?"

"She wants to put Mom and Auntie in jail."

"How did you put her to sleep?"

"I sprayed her face with motor spray."

"What is motor spray?"

"The stuff you spray in the weed whacker to get the motor to start."

"How did you know how to put her to sleep?"

"Mo said."

"Why did you take Detective Tindall's pants off?"

Mark smiled to himself briefly a couple of times. "She pooped in her pants." He snorted.

"Why did you let her go?"

"She said her kids needed her."

"Where can we find Mo?"

Mark looked confused. "I don't . . . I don't know. He just shows up at work sometimes."

"Does he have any friends that you know?"

"Jupe. Jupe the cop is his friend."

Karen ran out of the room with her phone.

Detective Devane said, "I think we're done for now. Thank you. This concludes the interview with Mark Breen."

FIFTY-FOUR

As Karen was driving back to Greenfield with Gil, her phone rang in the car speaker.

"Hey, Lili, what's up? I've got Gil here with me."

"Hi, guys. I don't have any ID for the lady we found at the fairgrounds, but we did get a match on the DNA from the gardening glove at the warehouse. Tina Renaldi, and she's also a match for DNA from the fairgrounds fire. She put her DNA on a commercial database only last week. I don't have any contact information."

"We know her! This is unbelievable. She's just a little old hippie lady that we interviewed."

"Thanks, Lili," said Karen. "I'll have her picked up." She drove the car to the side of the road and looked up Tina Renaldi's contact information, then called Chief Reyes to have the staties pick her up.

-When they got back to the station, they could hear raised voices coming from the chief's office. Karen asked one of the officers what was going on, and he told her that Reyes and Phillips were talking to Jupe. Karen went back to her desk. She felt more sad than angry.

Sitting next to her desk, Gil said, "I think the Tina Renaldi stuff is a frame-up. It's all too convenient and hard to believe at the same time."

Officer Jupe stormed out of the chief's office, his face bright red. He grabbed his jacket and left the station. Reyes and Phillips were talking with raised voices, then Phillips came out. He paused for a moment to compose himself, then he came

over to Karen's desk. "Jupe's suspended. I think he'll be fired."
He shook his head. "The guy pulling Breen's strings is named
Keith Moraine. Some people call him Mo. Others call him
Rain or Rainman. I'm going to go find him. Could you call the
staties and have them help me chase him down? Chief's busy
with the Jupe situation. I'll meet them at Susan Rassmussen's
antique shop."

"Got it. I'll see what I can find out about Moraine."

Phillips left to speak to one of the officers, then they left the
station.

"This Moraine guy may be the key! I wonder why he would
do this? I've got nothing to do, so I'm going to lunch," Gil said.
"Call me if you need me, but I'll be back in a little while."

"I'll want you there when Tina Renaldi's being
questioned."

"You got it."

————————

Gil went to the Mesa Verde restaurant and ordered a California
burrito and a limeade. The food was really good. He thought
about why this Moraine guy would do what he was doing.
Mark Breen seemed to be the only one with a motive. Maybe
Moraine was just screwing with the police. Maybe he had some
issue with them. Other than that, he could've just been evil and
treated these crimes like a game. Gil wasn't sure if that would
mean he was a sociopath or a psychopath.

It still didn't make sense that Tina Renaldi would be
involved. She was an artistic person from a peace-loving

commune that ended up helping abused women. But of course, he didn't know what he didn't know.

It was cold and windy, so he didn't want to walk around too much while he waited for Karen's call. Maybe he'd go look around in some shops. He finished eating, and as he left the restaurant, somebody with a strong arm grabbed him from behind and put a switchblade to his neck. Without thinking, Gil jerked his head back hard and clunked into his assailant's head. Then he backed up as hard and fast as he could. His assailant tripped over the stoop leading to the restaurant's door.

Gil could feel that his jaw had been slashed by the knife as he fell on top of his assailant, but he felt no pain. The assailant was stunned, and Gil got up and pounded on the glass door. Gil kicked his assailant's hand, and the knife clattered away. He could feel blood leaking down his neck. His assailant was a small young man. Moraine? His nose was gushing blood, and he was starting to move. Gil sat down hard on his belly.

Gil could hear a siren, and he hoped it was for him. His assailant was wriggling around, trying desperately to free himself. After a few minutes, which seemed like a very long time, a police car arrived, and the police yelled at Gil to put his hands on his head and step away from the other guy. An officer handcuffed Gil. The assailant scrambled to his feet. As the police told him to put his hands on his head, he bolted down the hill. One of the officers gave chase and quickly tackled him.

Another siren was approaching. The officer with Gil looked at him more closely and asked him if he was Mr. Novak. "Yes, my license is in my wallet. I think that guy is Moraine, the guy Sergeant Phillips is out looking for. His knife is under that plant over there."

He removed Gil's handcuffs while apologizing. "I just didn't recognize you with all the blood. I'm Officer O'Neill." He got Gil some paper towels from the restaurant and had him press the towels to his wound. The ambulance showed up, and the EMT had Gil sit on the ground while she checked him out. She bandaged the cut on his jaw as best she could, but she told him it was still oozing blood and he'd need to go to the ER to clean out the wound and get stitches. She offered him a ride in the ambulance, but he declined.

Another EMT told the officers that the assailant wasn't thinking too clearly and should get checked out at the ER for concussion. He recommended ambulance transport, just in case he went downhill. One of the officers accompanied their prisoner.

O'Neill reported Gil's version of the events on his radio, then he told Gil he'd take him to the ER after he talked to some witnesses.

Gil's jaw was starting to hurt a lot more. A few people had gathered to watch and one of them asked Gil what happened. Gil just said, "A guy jumped me with a knife, but I got him."

The guy grinned and said, "Right on, man," flashing Gil back to the hippie days.

FIFTY-FIVE

Gil was released from the ER with a big bandage covering his sixteen stitches. He opted for ibuprofen rather than opiates for the pain. Karen brought him back to the Mesa Verde restaurant so he could walk her through the incident. She couldn't help but laugh when he told her his ultimate hand-to-hand combat move of sitting real hard on his assailant.

"See," Gil said, "carrying a little extra weight *can* extend your life expectancy."

"The doc says that Mr. Moraine has a concussion, so you must have really headbutted him. They're keeping him overnight just to be safe, and we'll probably get to interview him tomorrow. Officer O'Neill says Moraine took off down the hill when he separated you guys."

"Yeah, that's right."

"Let's go have a look. Miles Street is a dead end. Maybe his vehicle is down here. Records show doesn't have a car of his own, but he has to have gotten there somehow."

"Company car?"

"Maybe. But which one?"

They walked down the street to a well-groomed area called Energy Park, which was a bit of a misnomer. Although there were a few solar panels to power the lighting, the real theme was trains. There was a train caboose, some playground trains for kids to play on, and even a train-station-shaped bandstand. Besides that, the whole area was surrounded by two sets of active train tracks, based on the warning signs. Nobody was there, probably because it was cold, and school was in session. "No vehicles parked down here," said Karen.

"He might have planned to hop the fences and cross the train tracks. Could be a lot to search."

Karen said, "Well, we'll try and figure out what he drives during our interrogation tomorrow."

Gil was in the little room behind the one-way mirror, looking into the interview room at the Greenfield Police Department. Detectives Devane and Tindall sat at the interview table opposite Keith Moraine and a young public defender named Shanice Davis.

"The court has arranged for you to have Ms. Davis as your defense attorney, as you requested," said Detective Devane. "Have you had sufficient time to meet with her before we begin?" Moraine nodded. "Please state your answers aloud so they can be recorded."

Moraine said, "Yes."

"Thank you. We've arrested Mark Breen and charged him with attempted kidnapping of a police officer, attempted murder of a member of the public, and several cases of arson. Are you acquainted with Mark Breen?"

"Yes."

"Have you discussed any of the crimes I mentioned with Mr. Breen?"

"No."

"Are you familiar with the case involving the kidnapping of Detective Tindall?"

Moraine looked over at Attorney Davis, who nodded. "Yes."

"How are you familiar with that case?"

"I heard about it. I heard it through the buzz."

"Who exactly told you about it?"

"I don't remember."

"Did you read about it, see it on the internet? TV news?"

"No, just through the buzz."

"What do you know about it?"

"That someone kidnapped Detective Tindall for a few days and that she was found safe in Turner's Falls."

"Anything else?"

"Don't answer that," said Attorney Davis. "Asked and answered."

Moraine chuckled. "She shit her pants."

Attorney Davis's eyes went wide. "Don't say anything if I object to the question."

"Do you know anything about the attempted murder of Mr. Gil Novak?"

"Yeah, I heard about it through the buzz."

"What do you know about it?"

"That the rope was too low, so it missed his neck."

Attorney Davis gave a momentary look of defeat. "I need five minutes to confer with my client."

Detective Devane suspended the interview, and he and Karen left the room. "All the news reports reported that it was a cable strung across the road," said Karen. "It was an error by a reporter. Moraine knew it was a rope."

Devane's face lit up. "Wouldn't Jupe have told him about the rope?"

"I don't think Jupe knows about the rope. The staties handled the crash." They went back in and restarted the interview.

"Do you know anything about the recent arsons in local schools?" Detective Devane asked.

"Yeah, I heard about them through the buzz."

"What do you know about them?"

"No comment," Moraine said.

"Why did you attack Gil Novak yesterday?"

"No comment."

Attorney Davis said, "Mr. Moraine has said all he's going to say about the crimes in question, so I think we're done here."

"Hold on," said Karen. "I have another question. Do you know a woman named Tina Renaldi?"

Moraine smiled. "No."

Detective Devane looked at Karen, who shrugged. "Very well," he said. "This concludes the interview. Keith Moraine, I am arresting you on suspicion of conspiracy in connection with the kidnapping of Detective Tindall, the attempted murder of Mr. Gil Novak, and recent arsons in this area." He had an officer take him to a jail cell.

FIFTY-SIX

Tina Renaldi had hired a defense attorney before sitting in the interview room early that evening. She was wearing a colorful blouse with an ankle-length, embroidered denim skirt.

"Ms. Renaldi, do you recognize this glove?" Karen asked.

"It looks like one of my gardening gloves. I've been looking for those!"

"Why have you been looking for them?"

"They've been missing for a few days. I could have sworn they were on my back porch with my gardening tools."

"When did you notice that they were missing?"

"I think it was last Thursday. I was going to pull up some more of my plants now that the frosts have arrived."

"Was anything else missing from your house?"

"No, I don't think so. Wait a minute, I lost my toothbrush and my hairbrush! I admit that I'm getting old, but how do you lose a toothbrush? It's always sitting in its holder in the bathroom. Luckily I had a spare that the dentist's office gave me. I'm always losing my hairbrush, though."

"When did you notice that your toothbrush was missing?"

"I don't remember what day it was. Sometime last week."

"Did you hear about my kidnapping recently?

"Yes, it was in the news. I'm glad you're all right. Why are you asking me these questions?"

"This glove was found at the scene of my kidnapping. How was your glove at the scene of my kidnapping?"

She looked at her lawyer, then back at Karen. "I . . . I have no idea. It looks like my missing glove, but why do you think it's mine?"

Karen pulled three DNA evidence reports from her file and placed them on the table, facing Tina and her lawyer. "This shows that your DNA was found on this glove from the scene of my kidnapping. This one shows that your DNA was found at the scene of a recent arson at the Franklin County Fairgrounds, in which a woman was seriously injured. This report confirms that it's your DNA because it matches your DNA profile in the 23andMe data repository. Why was your DNA found at the scene of an arson at the fairgrounds?"

Tina looked frantic. "It can't be! I don't have a profile on any DNA database. And I haven't been to the fair in years. Somebody must be framing me!"

Karen put a mugshot on the table and asked, "Do you know this man? His name is Keith Moraine, also known as Mo, Rain, and Rainman."

"No. I've never heard of him, and I've never seen him before."

Karen put another mugshot on the table. "Do you know this man? His name is Mark Breen."

"No, I've never heard of him or seen him before."

"Very well, that's all the questions I have. Ms. Renaldi, I am not charging you with any crimes at this stage of the investigation." Karen concluded the interview and stopped the recording. "I am requesting a swab sample of your DNA before you leave. I don't yet have a court order for this, but I can get one."

Tina looked at her lawyer who nodded. Tina agreed to the swab sample.

When they were done, Karen said, "Thank you, Ms. Renaldi. You are free to go."

Tina was clearly shaken by the whole experience.

FIFTY-SEVEN

Susan Rasmussen and Pam Leone drank coffee and waited anxiously with Karen, Lili, and Gil. The conference room at the *Greenfield Recorder* building was slightly too cold, which didn't help the jitters. Gil had swapped his large hospital bandage for several smaller, skin-tone ones. Kenny Tran opened the door, and Helene Faucher walked in hesitantly with a younger woman in a smart pantsuit. Helene and Susan burst into tears and hugged each other while Pam looked on nervously. A news photographer was quietly taking pictures in the background. Helene cupped her hands around Pam's face and said, "I see that you are my daughters, but I would never have recognized you! You're so beautiful!"

Kenny introduced himself and invited them all to sit. "Helene, this is Detective Karen Tindall, Forensic Scientist Lili D'Amico, and Mr. Gil Novak. They found your daughters."

"There are not enough words for my thanks," said Helene. "I thought I'd never see them again."

"I saw you," said Susan. "You had died! This is a miracle. All these years, I carried a big emptiness. But you didn't die that day. My God!"

Pam was shaking. She burst into tears, then buried her face in her hands. "You couldn't protect us!" She looked into Helene's eyes, her eyes red. "You couldn't save us from him!"

Helene put her hand on Pam's arm. "I know. I know I couldn't. I am so sorry. We all suffered so much."

After the family talked some more, the woman that had come in with Helene Faucher introduced herself as Olivia

Tremblay, a diplomat from the Canadian consulate in Boston. She asked, "Excuse me, but do you intend to interrogate Mademoiselle Faucher?"

"We've already interviewed Ms. Faucher remotely," said Detective Tindall. "We have no further need to question her. We provided a transcript of that interview to the New York State Police so they could close the file on their old assault and kidnapping case. We confirmed the death of Mr. Remi Foy, so there is no need to further pursue his crimes. Unfortunately, we have had to charge Ms. Faucher's grandson with crimes apparently associated with his attempts to protect his mother and his aunt from issues arising from the death of his brother Julian. However, neither Susan nor Pam appears to be involved in Julian's death, which may or may not have been accidental."

Ms. Tremblay said, "In that case, my services are no longer needed here. I wish you all the best." She took Helene's hand, whispered to her, and left.

A quiet descended upon the room. "There's one thing I don't understand in all of this," said Helene. "How did all of this come about so many years later?"

Karen looked at Gil.

"I guess this all happened because I got help for my insomnia," said Gil. "A lot of my sleep problems came from terrible nightmares I was having almost every night. I went to a doctor that hypnotized me, and it helped me remember an incident that happened when I was a teenager. I had climbed up the mountain here in town, and I was spying on this hippie family living in a cave."

Susan's eyes went wide. "You're that boy? The boy my father shot at?"

"Yep, that was me. When he shot at me, I ran as fast as I could, but I fell. I think I got knocked out. Anyway, I recently came back to Greenfield to try and find out about that, and it turned out that I was a witness to events surrounding the death of your child."

"So how did he die?" Pam asked. "How did Jules die?"

"I don't know. I didn't see what happened, or I don't remember it. I'm so sorry about all of that. But I'm glad you're all together again. And I'm sleeping much better!"

"This whole story is unbelievable!" said Helene, smiling. "Mr. Tran, none of this was in your newspaper article!"

"I didn't want your happy reunion story to be tied to the cold case involving your grandson Julian or the criminal cases involving your grandson," said Mark.

A look of shock came over Helene's face, and she put her hand over her mouth. "Theo, my God!" She looked around the room. "Until you said that, I never thought of Jules and Theo as my grandchildren. I thought of them as evil because they were the result of Remi's crimes. But they are my daughter's children. They are my grandchildren." She started weeping.

"There is something else you should know," said Lili. "Remi didn't die until 1996. He changed his name to Douglas Foy and was living in Maine." Susan, Pam, and Helene looked shocked. "Apparently he'd stopped drinking for a few years, remarried, and had three kids. Then he started up again, and his wife Regina left him and took the kids. Remi died a few years later of liver failure."

Nobody said anything for an uncomfortable moment.

"On a more positive note," said Gil, "you have two half brothers named Aaron and Christian and a half sister named

Carly. Lili and I met Aaron and his mother, Regina, and they are very nice people. Aaron asked if they could meet you. I can give you his contact information."

———————————

Gil walked over to Karen's desk to say goodbye. "What are those?" he asked.

"Those are pictures of Keith Moraine's truck. I took them when we brought him in for questioning."

"I recognize those button pins hanging from the rearview mirror. I remember them from when I was a kid." One of the buttons had a picture of the earth and said, "Stop the World, I Want to Get Off." The other had a picture of Alfred E. Neuman and said, "What, Me Work?"

"Who is that guy?" Karen asked.

"That's Alfred E. Neuman, the main character from *Mad Magazine*."

"I don't know what you're talking about."

"It was an old funny magazine from the sixties. But anyway, where's that picture of Sneaky Pete that you had from Social Services? I peeked at it while we were searching for you." Karen found the picture in her computer and pulled it up. Sneaky Pete was wearing a jacket full of button pins. Gil pointed. "See? Right there."

Karen's eyes lit up. "You may just have solved a murder or two."

"Well, that's good, I suppose. I'll see you later at dinner."

FIFTY-EIGHT

Gil and Lili arrived at the Greenfield Country Club and were shown to the banquet room where the others had gathered. "Apparently Mayor Jakobi is making this an opportunity to show off to other politicians," said Lili.

"As long as there's food, I'm okay with that. Everybody's taking a chance on COVID without their masks, though."

"Well, we only live once!" said Lili.

Karen made a beeline for them when they entered. "Hi, guys. Come with me." She dragged them over to a woman in a gray pantsuit with a dark blue blouse and an American flag lapel pin. "Mayor Martha, this is Lili D'Amico from the crime lab and Gil Novak, our consultant."

"I'm so pleased to meet you," said the mayor. "This is a great day for law enforcement! What a great example of state and city departments working together. Mr. Novak, I've heard all about your exploits here. It's an unbelievable story!"

"It hasn't all sunk in for me yet. But, it's been great to be back in my old stomping grounds."

Martha took his hand, winked at him, and said, "Well, maybe you'll move back to your stomping grounds. We could always use some more smart people."

"It's been an honor to meet you, Mayor," said Lily, then she steered Gil away. "Apparently I've got some competition."

Karen followed behind. "Oh, that's just Martha's way of getting votes. She's actually happily married, as far as I can tell. By the way, Social Services identified our burn victim as a homeless woman named Sharon Gilly. Her local nickname is Lightfoot, but nobody knows why. She's going to be okay."

Gil stopped and faced Karen. "There's one thing I still don't understand—well, maybe a lot of things. How did Mark Breen know who I was and that I'd be riding on Route 2 the day he almost killed me? And why was Moraine involved in any of these things at all?"

"Oh yeah, I forgot to tell you the rest of that story. You heard during Mark's interrogation that Moraine, who is Mark Breen's friend, is also a friend of Officer Jupe. It turns out that soon-to-be Ex-Officer Jupe was freely sharing information to impress his friends. When Dwayne and the chief questioned Jupe, he told them everything. Dwayne doesn't think he intended to help anybody commit a crime. It's too bad for Jupe. He didn't know the ramifications of his casual chats. As far as Keith Moraine's motive, I think he just thought of all these crimes as a game."

Gil laughed. "Dwayne? Dwayne Phillips? This is the first time I've heard that Sergeant Phillips had a first name!" Just then, Gil got a major slap on his back, causing him to cough hard. "Hi, Eddie."

"Gil Novak, I'd like to introduce you to my friend Pam Leone. Oh, but I hear you've already been spying on her and secretly meeting with her behind my back. Perhaps I should challenge you to a duel! Perhaps we should joust! Where are my gauntlets?"

Gil smiled. "Pam, it's so nice to meet you without all that formality going on. I feel like I've been dreaming about you my whole life." Pam looked confused. "This is Karen, and this is Lili. We've all been working on your case. Lili, this is Eddie Locke an old friend of mine and a friend of Pam's."

Pam said, "I'm so happy to meet you all. This whole situation is so confusing to me, especially meeting my mother again." Susan and Helene wandered over, and introductions were made. Pam asked, "So what did you mean about dreaming about me your whole life?"

During the party, Chief Reyes brought his people together. "I wanted to thank you all for pursuing this case. In the end, we never really figured out what happened to Julian Foy, but I don't think there are any more related threats out there. This investigation actually ended up encouraging more people to commit crimes, and we'll bring them to justice. We also solved some unrelated murders. Violence was committed against Gil and Karen, and I regret that. But I'm especially grateful to Gil for volunteering his help."

"I'm honored that I was able to help. This whole situation was really surreal. I think the best thing that came out of it was that we reunited a family that was torn apart so many years ago. I can't imagine what these girls are feeling."

Lili gave Gil a shove. "They're women, Gil, not girls! By the way, Pamela and Susan said that they're going to meet their half siblings from Maine. I think that would be a very intriguing discussion."

They stopped talking when Pam's band, Soundslip, started to play. Gil was transfixed by Pam's beautiful voice and stage presence. She chose a song called "Mother." He felt Lili looking up at his face, and he smiled.

FIFTY-NINE

It was still dark when Gil woke up, and he was confused about where he was. He saw a few red and green LEDs and light outlining the curtains. When his hazy brain cleared, he remembered where he was: a hotel in Yuma, Arizona. He pressed the button on his phone, which said 6:09 a.m.

Gil smiled, elated that he'd been sleeping soundly for the past few weeks. He'd been averaging six-and-a-half hours each night, and it felt amazing. He quietly got out of bed, being careful to let Lili sleep.

––––––––––––––

Gil and Lili pulled their motorcycles into the parking lot at the Belmont Pier in Long Beach, California. They removed their helmets and smiled at each other for having completed their three-week trek across the United States. They'd taken the southern route, following I-10 most of the way to avoid the cold winter weather to the north. They stowed their gear but kept their jackets on because of the cool west wind. They laughed, hugged each other, and held hands as they walked along the pier. Seagulls and pelicans sat on the railings where people were fishing, and a handful of surfers rolled over the waves in their wetsuits. Many cargo ships were anchored between the beach and the horizon, waiting to dock at the ports of Long Beach and Los Angeles.

When they got to the end, the pier broadened to a wide fishing area. A young couple came running over, and Amelia hugged her dad. Gil met her boyfriend, Owen, then introduced them to Lili. Amelia inspected the scar on Gil's jaw, jabbed him in the shoulder, smiled, and shook her head. Gil saw his late wife in Amelia when she smiled, and a flood of emotions overwhelmed him, causing him to tear up.

ACKNOWLEDGMENTS

I'd like to thank my wife Anne for being understanding and encouraging while I spent many hours writing. She also provided insightful editorial comments for this book.

The characters in this book are composites of my family, my friends, and my imagination. I'd like to specially acknowledge my sons Yli and Cael, my daughter-in-law Jessica, and my granddaughters Kaia and Mira for being great reference characters.

My editor, Jesse Winter from Duo Storytelling, was extremely helpful with his edits and thoughtful comments. He was very professional, encouraging, and a pleasure to work with.

I'd also like to acknowledge Draft2Digital for creating an amazing platform for self-publishing.

The wonderful cover design was created by johnny_an at 99Designs. This design used the following photographs:

Model skull of human and bones form pit with dark light by Suthiporn [1]at Adobe Stock. Cave-cavern-nature-stones-rocks by Dmitrijs Bojarovs at Pixabay. Foggy monsoon season in Mahabaleshwar, Maharashtra, India by artqu at Adobe Stock.

The author photograph was created by Erin Moore at Mercy Street Studio, Eliot, Maine.

I'd also like to acknowledge Draft2Digital for creating an amazing platform for self-publishing.

This book was written by a human.

---

1. https://stock.adobe.com/jp/contributor/207566155/suthiporn?load_type=author&prev_url=detail

Don't miss out!

Visit the website below and you can sign up to receive emails whenever Hy Shaw publishes a new book. There's no charge and no obligation.

https://books2read.com/r/B-A-LWEY-VTNIC

BOOKS 2 READ

Connecting independent readers to independent writers.

Ingram Content Group UK Ltd.
Milton Keynes UK
UKHW011610210623
423807UK00001B/13